EVEN WHEN YOUR VOICE SHAKES

EVEN WHEN
YOUR VOICE
SHAKES

Ruby Yayra Goka

ACCORD BOOKS

NORTON YOUNG READERS
An Imprint of W. W. Norton & Company
Independent Publishers Since 1923

Especially for Maya, Selasie, and Elike

For information about permission to reproduce selections from this book, write to Permissions, W. W. Norton & Company, Inc., 500 Fifth Avenue, New York, NY 10110

For information about special discounts for bulk purchases, please contact W. W. Norton Special Sales at specialsales@wwnorton.com or 800-233-4830

Manufacturing by Lakeside Book Company
Production manager: Beth Steidle

ISBN 978-1-324-01711-0

W. W. Norton & Company, Inc., 500 Fifth Avenue, New York, N.Y. 10110
www.wwnorton.com

W. W. Norton & Company Ltd., 15 Carlisle Street, London W1D 3BS

2 4 6 8 0 9 7 5 3 1

Speak the truth, even when your voice shakes.

—ANONYMOUS

CHAPTER 1

"I'm not going. Nothing you can say will make me change my mind." Amorkor's breath hitched as she tried very hard to keep the tears from flowing down her face. She folded her arms and turned her face away from me. Though she had bathed, she was still in her house clothes.

Tsotsoo's lower lip had begun to tremble. She scrunched up her face and let out a wail. "Sister Amerley, me too, I won't go. They'll just send us back for school fees."

We were in front of our single room in the compound house we shared with nine other families. The compound was made up of three semidetached one-room buildings along each of the three fence walls. Our landlord's three-bedroom house, complete with indoor bath, kitchen, and toilet, made up the last wall. Each of the single units was the same: walls badly needing paint, torn mosquito nettings, warped front doors opening onto the one room for living, sleeping, and storage. We all shared a communal bathroom. There was no toilet.

1

A cashew tree stood in the center of the compound. It served as our community center. It was where the landlord met with our parents, neighbors caught up on gossip and life in the evenings, and the children played in the afternoons. All around us, our neighbors were in various stages of getting ready to leave for school or work. Chickens were foraging in the red soil for insects. Someone had cut plantain leaves for the goats and hung them on the cashew tree.

Earlier, I'd been admiring the swirly pattern our brooms had made on the red soil. It was our week to sweep the compound, and though my sisters and I had done a good job, goat droppings now littered most of the compound. I rubbed my forehead. My head was pounding and it was just seven in the morning. I couldn't seem to focus on anything with this headache. I'd been up since dawn fetching water for my family and one of the neighbors. The taps had been off for five days. Our neighbor had given me five cedis for the fifteen buckets I'd carried to fill the water drum in the corner of her veranda. Since my mother, Amerley-mami, no longer worked, we couldn't afford to buy water from the water tankers.

I'd used that money I'd earned to buy *koko*, a thick maize porridge, and *koose*, fried bean cakes, for my sisters. My head was threatening to split open, the pounding in tandem with my heartbeat. The left part of my head felt like it was caught in a vise. My sister's cries were making it worse.

"Listen, today is the first day of school. No one will send

you back because of school fees." I shut my eyes and tried to will the pain away. What I'd said was the truth. No one would send my sisters home for fees on the first day of school. I knew that firsthand. I'd been sent home for school fees all my life. Never on the first day, though; it was usually during midterms or just before our end-of-term exams.

Amorkor lost the battle with her tears and they flowed down her face as if a dam somewhere within her had burst open, and maybe it had. We had had a terrible Christmas. There'd been no new clothes or shoes. No cookies or soft drinks. No *jollof* rice or chicken. Nothing. Christmas had passed like any other day. New Year's Day had been better. We had heard one of the big churches was sharing packed lunches for *kayayei* and their children. We'd joined the thousands of street children and head porters on the streets that morning and had come home with mismatched *fos* clothes and packs of fried rice with three pieces of gizzard and a bottle of Coke each. It didn't matter that the clothes were used, were several sizes too big, and smelled like mothballs, or that the fried rice had begun to go slimy. I was just thankful that we'd had food to eat that day. As for our clothes, I was good with a thread and needle—I would do the necessary adjustments and at least my sisters would have decent clothes to wear.

"I'm not going," Amorkor said again.

Tsotsoo's wails went up a notch higher in solidarity.

"What is going on here? Can't we have any peace in this house?

What's all this crying for?" Nuumo shouted from his home across the courtyard. He was in a pair of khaki shorts and an undershirt that looked more yellow than white. At the sight of Nuumo, both Amorkor and Tsotsoo stopped their tears. He broke off a twig from the neem tree beside his house, stripped the bark, and stuck it into his mouth.

"Aren't you girls going to school? What are you still doing here when your friends are already on their way? Do you want to be late on the first day?"

My sisters scurried off to get dressed before Nuumo was even done with his questions. He was walking toward us. He had softened the ends of the neem twig and was using it to clean his teeth.

"Good morning, Nuumo," I greeted him.

"Don't 'good morning' me. Where's my money?"

He had stopped asking where my parents, Amerley-mami and Ataa, were months ago.

I stood there silent. I'd run out of excuses and he knew it.

"If I don't have my money by six p.m., I'll have no choice but to evict you tomorrow. There are two families who are ready to pay me two years' advance. I also have a family to feed. Tonight. Six p.m." He hacked up a glob of yellowish phlegm and spat it at my feet.

I sank onto a stool by our door and rested my head on the wooden pane. Where was I going to get the rent money from?

My three sisters came out. They were all dressed and ready to go. Though their uniforms were old, they were clean and ironed. I sat up straight and forced a smile onto my face. I don't know where Amarkai had managed to get the stale bread from, but she held a piece in her hand. The minute the animals saw her, they ran toward us. She broke off pieces of moldy bread for the chickens and goats. The dogs just wanted to be petted.

"I'll get the money for your fees by the end of the week."

My sisters had skeptical looks on their faces. Even Tsotsoo, who was only six.

"I promise."

"That's what you said before Christmas," Amorkor said.

"It's true. Madam Fosua owes me money. When I went to her house, they said she'd gone to her hometown for the holidays. She should be back this week."

Amorkor sniffed and wiped her nose with the back of her hand. Tsotsoo was looking at Amorkor to decide what to do next. I gave them each a one-cedi note as their lunch money. Amorkor picked up her bag and walked out of the courtyard. Tsotsoo did the same.

"What about the rent?" Amarkai asked when Amorkor and Tsotsoo were out of hearing range.

I offered her a weak smile. "I'll figure it out. Don't worry."

"But Nuumo said—"

"Don't worry about Nuumo. You'll be late if you don't hurry."

There was still a look of doubt on her face as she chased Amorkor and Tsotsoo. Tsotsoo turned and gave me one last wave before the three of them disappeared from view.

Tsotsoo is still the baby of the family. She almost lost her place six months ago when Mama delivered a baby girl. Unfortunately, the baby was stillborn. If she had lived she would have been called Fofo. I think Fofo is such a lovely name. Both my parents are Ga, so there was no dispute over our names. My clan has two sets of names that male members use alternately between generations for their children. Because of this, every man knows the names of all his prospective children. A man takes his grandfather's names for his children, and his grandsons take his name for their children. We are also named according to our positions of birth. I'm Naa Amerley because I'm the first girl. Next is Naa Amorkor, then Naa Amarkai, then Tsotsoo, who really should have been called Naa Amatsoo. Naa is because we are female. A boy would be Nii. The suffixes *-ley, -okor, -kai, -tso,* and *-fo* for the first five females, and the suffixes *-te, -tei, -twei, -ai,* and *-yi* for the first five males. It's a bit confusing, but among Gas, once you mention your name everyone knows which clan you're from and your hierarchy in the birth order.

If Fofo had been born a boy, she would have been called Nii Armah. Ataa, my father, did not hide the fact that he'd hoped

Fofo would be a boy. In fact, he'd hoped we all had been born boys. When he'd been told the baby was a stillborn girl, he'd slammed his fist into the wall at the maternity clinic. Ataa used to be a bodybuilder when he was younger. He had let himself go and had developed a paunch but he was still strong. He'd done some major damage to that wall, but the nurses were too scared to say anything. I'd thought he'd been upset that the baby was dead. I was wrong. He'd stormed into the ward where my mother was lying in bed. I had followed from a safe distance—crossing my father when he was angry was never a good idea.

"What's wrong with you?" he'd screamed. "What type of woman are you? Why can't you give me sons?"

Amerley-mami had sobbed into her pillow. Everyone calls my mother Amerley-mami, even me. That's also a Ga thing. A woman becomes known by the name of her first child after birth. It was while I was standing there that I remembered what had happened six years earlier. I'd been at school when my aunt, Auntie Odarkor, had come for Amorkor, Amarkai, and me.

"You have a new sister," she had said, her eyes sparkling. She had taken us to the maternity clinic where Amerley-mami was cradling Tsotsoo in the crook of her arm. My sisters and I had watched our beautiful baby sister as she slept. Amorkor and Amarkai soon lost interest in Tsotsoo and went out to play.

In no time at all I heard Amarkai shout, *"Onu mars, get set, pi."*

Almost immediately Amorkor started shouting, "Cheater!

Cheater! You started running before you said '*pi*.' I won't play again."

I stayed by Amerley-mami's bedside watching her and my new sister sleep, so it was I who saw Ataa when he walked into the room. He reeked of cigarettes and *akpeteshie*. He hadn't come bearing gifts, but I was sure he had already spent a small fortune on the locally brewed gin. Ataa is a fisherman, so he walks with a rolling gait even when he is on land. His movements that day were more clumsy and unsteady. He took two steps into the room and stopped in front of the door.

"Look, a new baby," I'd squealed.

"Another girl!" he'd slurred, and lumbered out of the room. He hadn't even gone to see Tsotsoo. He hadn't come home that night. He hadn't come home a week later when it was time to name Tsotsoo, so her naming ceremony was postponed. Ataa didn't even send her a cloth. In our culture when a baby is born, the father has to send the child a cloth to keep it warm. Sending a cloth demonstrates that he is ready and willing to take on the responsibility of looking after the child. I'm not sure anyone sticks to that anymore, so Ataa could have been forgiven for not sending a cloth. What he shouldn't have been forgiven for was not showing up on the day of Tsotsoo's naming ceremony.

Because he didn't show up, the ceremony wasn't performed and Tsotsoo was not named Naa Amatsoo. And because we couldn't just keep calling her "Baby" forever, my grandmother, whom we all call Awo, started calling her Tsotsoo. It was only Ataa who had the right to name her Naa Amatsoo. He never did. He came home two months after Tsotsoo's birth. When Amerley-mami asked him about Tsotsoo's naming ceremony, he hit her so hard she couldn't walk for two weeks. She never brought it up again.

Ataa took to disappearing for months on end when Fofo died. Even when things had been good between him and Amerley-mami, we were used to him being gone days at a time on his fishing expeditions. Most of the time my sisters and I were glad that he was gone. When he was home, we had to be extra quiet because he slept during the day. He didn't pay any particular attention to us when he was awake. He only took notice of us when he needed someone to send a bucket of water to the bathroom or to buy him cigarettes and *akpeteshie* from Daavi's kiosk down the road. We heard he was shacked up with a divorcée who had twin boys in the next town. Some also said he had moved in order to become a land guard for some chiefs at Kasoa. Wherever he was, he hadn't sent word to us. We didn't even know if he was still alive.

CHAPTER 2

I sat back on the stool and tried to figure out what to do. It was true Madam Fosua owed me money. I had done her laundry for her a few months back. But the money she owed me wouldn't be enough for the rent, let alone my sisters' school fees. Now that school had reopened, there were all these other costs that came with it—books, classes fees, feeding fees, money for Wednesday worship, and who knew what else.

On days like this, it was easy to feel overwhelmed. It was easy to want to give up and just stay in bed and pretend our problems did not exist, which was exactly what Amerley-mami was doing. I felt tears burning in my eyes but I blinked them back. Crying was pointless. I had to do something and I had to do it fast. I couldn't go to any of our neighbors. Now that schools had reopened, none of them would have any money to spare, let alone to pay rent for six months. I pushed myself off the stool and went inside the room. It took a minute for my eyes to get accustomed to the darkness. The girls had rolled up our mattresses and stacked them in the corner.

The four armchairs that made up our living room set were still in the other corner, where we had pushed them to make way for our mattresses the night before. I found some acetaminophen tablets they had given Amerley-mami when she first came back from the hospital. I took two of them and chased them down with a cup of water.

My sisters and I slept on two mattresses on the floor of our living room. A curtain separated the living room from my parents' sleeping area. When Ataa was at home, the curtain remained down at night and Tsotsoo and I shared one mattress and Amorkor and Amarkai the other. We heard, or rather *I* heard, since my sisters were always fast asleep by that time, everything that went on behind the curtain when my father was home. Everything. Ataa being away meant that Tsotsoo and Amarkai got to sleep on the big bed with Amerley-mami, which also meant that Amorkor and I had our mattresses all to ourselves. When it was just Amerley-mami and us, we would leave the curtain open so that what little breeze came into the room from her side of the room would circulate in the living room where we slept.

Amerley-mami's still form lay on the bed. She had been in the same nightie for almost a month. She sometimes got out of bed at night to pee and drink some water and to eat whatever food I'd left her. Her hair was matted and it stank. I don't remember the last time she'd had a bath. She avoided our neighbors. No one came to check on her anymore.

"Amerley-mami, Nuumo asked for the rent again," I said, shaking her when I got close to her bed. She was lying on her side with a faraway look in her eyes. She gave no indication she had heard me.

"Amerley-mami, say something. He said he'll evict us if we don't pay him by six tonight." Tears had pooled in my eyes but again I refused to cry. "You have to do something. I'm tired of begging him. I don't know what to do anymore. It's not just him. We owe almost everyone in the house and the girls haven't paid their school fees. They started school today and Amorkor is already asking for her fees. Don't you care anymore? Don't—"

Amerley-mami turned away from me and faced the wall.

I couldn't keep it in any longer. I burst into tears beside my mother but she didn't budge. The pounding in my head got even worse. I wished my parents cared just a little bit. I wished my relatives didn't have their own problems and could help us. I lay on the floor beside my mother's bed for about an hour hoping she would say something. Do something. My mother didn't move a limb. A heaviness had settled on my chest: if I didn't do anything, my sisters and I would end up as street kids. I don't think Amerley-mami cared if she lived or died. Sometimes I thought we'd come home to find her lifeless body on the bed. I thought she'd given up.

I got up and checked on my mother. Her eyes were closed and she was breathing evenly. I envied her ability to sleep in the midst

12

of all we were going through. I envied how she could just shut everything out and pretend nothing was happening to us.

I went out of the room. The yard was quiet. The animals lay under the cashew and neem trees. Nuumo had his radio tuned to one of the morning shows and they were discussing corruption in the current government. I went out of the compound and down one of the alleys. There were few streets in our part of the neighborhood; the houses were built so close together that only footpaths separated them. The houses were all badly in need of paint, with rusted corrugated roofing sheets that leaked when it rained, torn mosquito netting, and verandas that served as both storage areas and kitchens. Most of the compounds had fruit trees—usually mango or orange, in which chickens roosted. Makeshift pens were made for sheep and goats. During the day they were set free to roam for their food. At night they made their way back to their homes to sleep. Life in this community was a struggle for all living creatures, not just humans.

I took a shortcut through someone's compound and arrived at Madam Fosua's house. She lived on the other side of town, which was a little more affluent than where we lived. That neighborhood had well-demarcated streets, and a few of the homeowners even had their own cars. She lived in a two-bedroom self-contained house with her husband, three kids, and a house help. She had been a good customer of Amerley-mami, who used to supply her with the fresh fish Ataa caught. Though she had a house help, she agreed to pay me to wash her clothes and run errands for her when I first went to ask her for a loan. I think she felt sorry for us.

"*Agoo*," I called out.

"*Amee*," Madam Fosua called from inside the house.

I sighed in relief. At least she was back from her hometown.

"Amerley, it's you," she said, coming out. She was an obese woman and she was always in a *boubou*. Her house help came out as well, with Madam Fosua's toddler son strapped to her back. The help looked at me like I was a nuisance. I ignored her and turned to Madam Fosua, who was locking their front door.

"Good morning, auntie."

"Good morning, my child. How are you?"

"I'm fine."

"And your sisters?"

"They're fine, auntie."

"And your mother?"

"She's there. Auntie, please, do you have a job for me?"

Madam Fosua turned to look at me. I don't know what she saw in my face, but I felt like she was looking right through me. Like she could tell I was about to ask her for a loan.

"Sorry I couldn't settle with you before going to the village." She opened her handbag, took out her purse, and pulled out a twenty-cedi note. "Now is not a good time for me. Schools have reopened and I have to buy fresh stock for my shop."

"Thank you," I said, taking the money and stuffing it into my bra.

"Auntie, our landlord is evicting us. We have nowhere to go."

"Amerley, I've already told you, now is not a good time. Where do you want me to get money from to pay rent for your family? Where is your father?"

I had no answers to her questions.

She opened her purse and pulled out another twenty-cedi note. "Manage with this okay? I'll ask around and let you know if anyone needs help with anything, but don't get your hopes up. Times are hard."

I nodded and thanked her again for the money.

"Greet your mother for me when you go home."

"Yes, auntie."

I walked beside her to the sidewalk where her help had flagged down a taxi. Madam Fosua climbed into the front seat. The car dipped visibly when she sat down. The help, with the child still strapped on her, settled in the back.

Next stop was the *trotro* station where my best friend, Sheba, and my boyfriend, Nikoi, worked. It was rush hour and long lines of people were waiting for the rickety commercial buses. Hawkers peddled items from handcarts or trays balanced on their heads to the early morning commuters. I waved at the *koko* seller I had bought my sisters' maize porridge from. Hot beverage, *waakye*, and *kenkey* sellers did a brisk business as people bought their breakfast. In one corner of the station, a preacher had set up a speaker and an offertory basket. Some people dropped money into it as they walked by him.

Nikoi and Sheba were both school dropouts like me. Nikoi worked as a driver's *mate*. Sheba hawked whatever fruit was in season—orange, pineapple, banana, pawpaw, mango, sugarcane, anything that she could sell and make a reasonable profit on. At night she sold pure water packets at the night market. She was pregnant and had been sick for a couple of weeks.

I spotted Sheba right away. You could already see her baby bump. She saw me and headed over.

"Amerley, what is wrong?" She lowered her tray of pawpaw from her head and sat beside me on a bench beneath a mango tree.

"I need money, Sheba. Nuumo says he'll kick us out of the house if we don't pay our rent by this evening."

"How many months do you owe?"

"Our two years were up in December. He says he has people willing to pay him two years' advance. Last year he told me we could pay six months' advance instead of the two years when I went to beg him to consider our situation."

"How much is it?"

I mentioned the amount.

"*Buei!*" Sheba shouted, and put her hands on her head. A few people threw curious glances in our direction. "Where are you going to get that type of money from?"

A lump formed in my throat and my vision got blurry. "I'm so scared," I sobbed as my best friend drew me in for a hug. "What are we going to do? We have nowhere to go."

"Have you tried calling your father?"

I nodded. "First his phone was always out of coverage, and then the last two times I tried, they said the phone number doesn't exist."

"Do you want us to go and look for him in Nungua? I heard he's staying with some Ewe woman there."

"Nikoi went to look for him before Christmas. He couldn't locate the house and no one seemed to know of him."

"How about Kasoa?"

I shook my head. "What's the point? Do you think he'll suddenly grow a conscience when he's abandoned us for six months? He knew the tenancy agreement would expire in December before he left. He knew the girls were in school. He didn't even leave chop money for us to buy food. How does he think we're surviving?"

"How about your mother?"

"She's nothing but a coward," I said, my temper rising. "All she does is stay in bed. At night when she thinks we're all asleep, she wakes up and drinks soakings. She just ignores us during the day." I didn't mind that she soaked *gari* in water for her meals, but the amount of sugar she used was more than my three sisters consumed for their morning porridge. She knew we had to be frugal with everything. Even sugar.

Sheba continued rubbing my back. "I thought she was sick."

I sniffed and dried my face. "I used to think so too. But she isn't. I mean, she doesn't have a fever and doesn't vomit or anything. I thought she was just sad when she lost the baby, but it's been six months. Does the dead baby mean more to her than us, her four healthy children?"

"Last time at the prenatal clinic, they were telling us some mothers get depressed after they have their babies. They can even get sad when the baby is healthy and fine and everything is all right. They said it's a mental illness. Maybe that's what is wrong with your mother. Maybe she should see a doctor."

I laughed. It was a laugh full of bitterness. "Will she pay the doctor with mango leaves?"

Sheba was quiet for a moment. "How about the alterations you do?"

I earned money by doing alterations to clothes, sewing on buttons and mending socks for our neighbors. It was tiring work since I didn't have a sewing machine and had to do it all by hand. On good days when I had customers I stayed up all night sewing. Amerley-mami couldn't sleep with the lights on, so I had to make do with candles. I pricked myself with the needle so many times that my fingers became numb, and some nights I had to force myself to stop because my eyes hurt. I was far cheaper than the seamstresses and tailors in the neighborhood, most of whom hated doing alterations to clothes. I accepted whatever money I was given. Sometimes people even gave me their used clothes, which I altered for my sisters and me. That saved me from worrying about how to clothe my sisters.

All my life, my dream was to become a seamstress and have my own shop. After junior high school, I'd done one term of senior high school before I dropped out because Amerley-mami had said there was no money to pay my fees. I'd asked to be enrolled as an apprentice to one of the seamstresses in our neighborhood. The woman operated out of a used metal shipping container and had a glass display with two mannequins. Anytime I had to run an errand, I made sure I passed in front of her shop just to see what styles her mannequins were wearing, even though it meant jumping over a large, stinking gutter filled with black polyethylene bags and pure water and yogurt packets, all of which swam in a river of black water.

When Amerley-mami had asked about enrolling me as an apprentice, the woman had given her a list of things I was supposed to buy and a cash amount. The items included a Singer sewing machine, a pack of twelve different-colored spools of thread, five pairs of scissors, three tape measures, ten yards of brown paper, five packs of pins, and five packs of needles. In addition to that, I was supposed to pay for two uniforms to be sewn for me. There was no way Amerley-mami could have afforded those items. She had told me to ask my father for the money the next time I saw him. I knew better than that. Ataa had stopped giving me money from the time Tsotsoo was born.

"I just do simple alterations. The money I make is not enough to pay six months' rent or school fees. That's what I use to feed us."

Sheba was quiet for a moment as she considered my options. She brightened and said, "You can sleep on our veranda. I'll ask Maame. I'm sure she wouldn't mind. They gave me a mosquito net to use when I went for my prenatal visit. We can string it up on the veranda for you guys."

"Does she have a kiosk now? Where will she run her business from?" Sheba's mother was a hairdresser. She braided and permed hair on her veranda.

"When she finishes with her customers, we'll just move all her things to one side and then you can sleep on the other side."

I sighed. Sleeping on Sheba's veranda was not the best option, but it beat sleeping out on the streets. At least we'd have a roof over our heads and we'd be safe. The tightness in my chest eased, and for the first time that morning I felt a ray of hope. I'd just have to work harder at finding a job. I stood up and scanned the *trotros* in the yard. Nikoi's was not among them.

"Nikoi's not back yet. His *trotro* was one of the first to load this morning," Sheba said, following my gaze.

"I better go and start packing. When the girls come home, we'll start moving our things."

Sheba gave me a last hug. "It will all work out. You'll see."

CHAPTER 3

I ignored Amerley-mami when I got home and upended our "Ghana-must-go" bags onto the center table. The bags got their name in the eighties when a Nigerian president ordered Ghanaians living in Nigeria without the necessary documentation to leave the country or be arrested. Most of the returnees returned to the shores of Ghana with their possessions packed into cheap nylon bags. The blue and white or red and white checked bags have no brand name and come in all sizes.

We didn't have any dressers. We kept all our clothes in the bags. We just stuffed them in after taking them off the beach sand, where we spread them out to dry after washing. I began folding the clothes into tight bundles and packing them in. Sheba's veranda was their kitchen as well, so we would not have enough space for all our things. Maybe I could ask Madam Fosua to keep the bigger items like Amerley-mami's bed and mattress and our living room furniture for us, or maybe we could sell them if we found a buyer—they weren't in very good condition.

I was so engrossed in my task I didn't notice our door had opened and someone was standing in front of me. I stifled a scream before I realized it was Nikoi. No one would call Nikoi good looking. He was taller than me but had an unremarkable face. But what he lacked in looks he more than made up for in the way he cared for my sisters and me.

He jerked his head in the direction of Amerley-mami's bed. A question. The curtain separating the two halves of the room was down and he couldn't tell if she was in or not. I nodded. Yes, she was in.

"I came as quickly as I could, but I have to get back soon," he whispered, and offered me his hand. A big callused hand that was spattered with what looked like engine oil. I took it anyway and let him lead me out of the room. The relief I felt was immediate. For the first time the entire day, I felt sure things would work out. Nikoi did that to me. He always put things into perspective and gave me hope.

"Sheba told me what happened. Today has been crazy. Schools have reopened and the traffic is terrible. Sorry I couldn't get here sooner."

"It's okay. Sheba sorted us out. We'll sleep on her veranda until . . ." I shrugged. I didn't know what the next step would be.

He squeezed my hand and led me out of the compound and through the narrow alleys that ran between the houses, toward the beach. We didn't speak as we headed to our spot—an isolated grove of coconut trees on the far side of the beach. Fishermen worked beneath some trees mending their fishing nets and tending to their canoes. The fishmongers were long gone, the day's harvest of fish having already been haggled over and sold. The sea sent out a salty spray as waves crashed onto the beach. Seagulls squawked as they chased each other above us. Young children who had skipped school played, turning cartwheels or competing in races. They didn't seem to mind that their hair and bodies were covered completely in the white sand. A group of young men harvested coconuts. Two of them had climbed the trees and were hacking off the fruits with cutlasses, while the others were filling their wheelbarrows with the greenish-yellow fruits. It was windy and I had to keep one hand on my skirt to keep the gusts from lifting it up and flashing my underwear. Nikoi's T-shirt billowed behind him like some sort of cape.

Nikoi kept turning to look at me, as if to make sure I was all right. Each time he turned, the sun glinted off the simple gold necklace he wore around his neck. It was the only thing he had left of his mother. She had died giving birth to his brother. His brother had survived the birth but died of malaria at age five. It wasn't something Nikoi talked about much.

I squeezed his hand to let him know I was all right.

We sank onto the sand when we got to our spot. He held me against him and kissed my forehead. Then he put his hand into his pocket and handed me an envelope. I opened it to find a bundle of money.

I looked up at him in confusion. "Nii, what—? How?"

"I've been saving to buy you the things you need so you could start your apprenticeship with that lady. I was hoping to have the full amount by Easter. Use that for the rent."

For the third time that day, I broke into tears. The tears came hot and fast down my face, and all Nikoi did was hold me and stroke my back just like Sheba had. I was not a pretty crier. My eyes always got red and my face got blotchy. I knew I looked a sight.

"Thank you," I said finally. I wiped my nose with the hem of my dress. "I didn't even know you'd been saving for me. I'll pay you back. I promise. One day I'll pay you back."

Nikoi tipped my head up so I could see into his brown eyes, and the corner of his lip lifted in a smile. "You're my girl. If I don't look after you, who will?"

I shook my head. "My sisters and I are not your responsibility. You shouldn't be sacrificing so much for us."

He shrugged. "You're my family. You're all the family I've got, and one day this will not be our life. I promise."

Nikoi's father was alive but they were estranged. Most of the time, he was dead drunk in the corner of the *akpeteshie* kiosk. Even when he was sober, he was always at the *akpeteshie* kiosk calculating lotto numbers and drinking the gin on credit. On one occasion when he'd been sober, he had thrown Nikoi out of the house after Nikoi had gotten into a fight with his stepmother.

I buried my face in Nikoi's chest and tried to will that future to come as soon as it could. That day when we would be in our own home with our own family. When I wouldn't have to worry about rent or school fees or where our next meal was coming from. When I'd have my own dressmaking shop and several apprentices and Nikoi would own a fleet of taxis.

Nikoi was the first to pull apart. He wiped the tears from my face with his greasy hands. "I have to get back now. I'll see you in the evening."

"Okay," I whispered as he slipped away.

CHAPTER 4

Though our rent had been paid up for the next three months, Nuumo reminded me every week that he expected the payment for the next one and a half years by the end of April. It was a worry I pushed aside. The more pressing issue for me was how to pay Amorkor and Tsotsoo's school fees. I did all the odd jobs I could find in addition to the alterations on clothes the neighbors brought in.

"You'll go blind one day if you keep doing this," Sheba remarked one evening when she saw me sewing by candlelight. She'd come to borrow some corn dough. Going blind was out of the question, so I cut back on the night sewing.

Every morning when I woke up I thanked God that at least I didn't have to worry about Amarkai's fees. Amarkai and Tsotsoo looked nothing like Amorkor or me. They both got our mother's beauty (though if you looked at Amerley-mami now, you couldn't tell how beautiful she had once been), whereas Amorkor and I would be mistaken for boys if we didn't wear earrings. We looked like Ataa would have looked if he were a girl. Amarkai wasn't even a teenager yet, but boys turned and stared whenever she walked past. Fortunately, she had no time for boys. Yet. All she cared about were animals. If there was a wounded cat or dog, a crippled chicken, or any sick animal, it was Amarkai people brought it to. When strands of wig blew from Sheba's mother's veranda as she braided rasta for women in the neighborhood, Amarkai chased their chickens and removed the strands from around their feet. The hairs would circle the chickens' feet and make them swell up. Sometimes they could even lose a foot.

Amarkai used to spend her weekends driving away the neighborhood boys who shot down birds with their catapults. Now she spent her weekends working at the veterinary clinic at La. She walked to and from the vet's. She didn't even get paid for the cleaning she did, but the vet paid her fees and bought her school supplies. Even if the vet was not taking care of her education, Amarkai would still have done the cleaning up just so she could watch while the vet took care of the sick animals. Amarkai and her animals were something out of a fairy tale. At around 3 p.m. all the animals in the neighborhood, both the strays and those with owners, marched to the roadside to wait for her. It became so normal that only visitors to the neighborhood got alarmed at all the different kinds of animals waiting at the bus stop in the afternoons. Usually by 3:15 p.m., Amarkai alit from the *trotro*.

As soon as she got off the bus, the animal chorus began. The dogs barked in greeting, the cats meowed in welcome, and the chickens and ducks did a welcome dance by ruffling their feathers. There used to be a sheep and he bleated anytime he saw her, until he was killed for Eid al-Adha. Because of this, people in the area brought her leftovers for the animals. At first, some mothers refused to let their children play with her because they said she had magical powers, but as time went on people realized that she just really, really loved animals. A TV station carried a story on her after someone saw the animals still waiting for her even though it was raining. People had gotten so used to seeing her with them that it wasn't a big deal anymore.

No matter how little her pocket money was, she always reserved some to buy a cob of maize or *kanzo* for the animals from the rice and *waakye* sellers. The food vendors had come to know her so well that they sometimes gave her those burnt portions for free. She held the food and stood there while the animals ate straight from her hand. I sometimes wondered how we could even be related!

Two years ago when Amarkai was attending the same school as my sisters and me, we came home to find Sheba and her little sister, Vashti, waiting for us on our veranda. Vashti had a Key Soap box on her lap, and we could see she had been crying. Sheba pulled Amarkai and me aside.

"It's her kitten; it's not eating. When we force-feed it, everything just comes out. It can't swallow. I think it's going to die," Sheba said.

Amarkai dropped her bag onto the ground and walked to where Vashti sat. She knelt in front of her and picked up the kitten.

"She'll be fine, she'll be fine," Amarkai said, stroking the brown and black ball of fur.

"I didn't know where else to go. Vashti has refused to eat anything. She just cries and cries and my mother is getting annoyed."

I saw how Vashti looked at Amarkai with wide eyes full of hope. You'd have thought Amarkai was one of those televangelists who make cripples walk. Tears streaked down Vashti's face and snot ran out of her nose. She was the same age as our Tsotsoo. She was nodding at something Amarkai was telling her. She wiped her nose and her face with the back of her hand.

"You leave her with me and go home. Make sure you eat because when she comes back she'll want to play with you. And feed her mother too; this little kitten will be starving when she gets better," Amarkai said.

"You promise she'll be fine?"

"I promise."

A wide smile broke out on Vashti's face. She stroked the kitten once more and put her hand in Sheba's. "Let's go, I'm hungry."

As I watched them walk away, I wondered what Amarkai was going to do. She had obviously bitten off more than she could chew this time. I knew she could splint broken legs and wings, but how could she make an animal eat that was refusing to?

I had left Amarkai with the kitten and went indoors to change and get supper ready. Amorkor had milled the maize we had soaked in the basin overnight, but instead of mixing it with water she had left the milled bowl of maize like that and had probably gone off somewhere to read. I didn't even bother looking for her. No one knew her hiding place. When Amorkor began reading a book, she wasn't any good to anyone until she was done.

Amarkai had found an eyedrop bottle, which she was washing out.

"What's that for?" I asked as I poured water onto the maize powder and kneaded it. I loved the feel of the warm corn powder on my hands as I mixed it.

"To feed the kitten."

"What's the point of having a bottle if you don't have milk?" I asked as I patted the dough and covered the bowl with its lid. It would ferment for two days and then we could begin using it for *banku*.

Amarkai rolled her eyes and showed me a packet of powdered milk. I didn't even know when she had gone to buy it. She mixed a quarter of the contents and put it into the eyedrop bottle. She tried feeding the kitten but the milk came back out a minute after it had swallowed it.

"Some of the milk stays down. She doesn't vomit it all. At least some stays in her stomach," she said after examining the milk.

Two days later the situation hadn't changed. The kitten's meowing was driving us crazy. Its cries were weaker and it wasn't moving at all. Amerley-mami told Amarkai to return the kitten before it "died on her." After school that day, Amarkai took the box and disappeared. I'd thought she had gone to return Vashti's kitten, so at 6 p.m. when she wasn't back I went to Vashti's house to look for her, only to be told she hadn't been there the entire day. I went back home, but didn't tell Amerley-mami. Amarkai came home at 7:30 p.m. with the kitten in the box.

When I asked where she'd been, she said she'd walked to the La Veterinary Center to beg the doctors to operate on the kitten. They'd told her the cost of the surgery would be one hundred cedis. She'd sat in the reception area and refused to leave until the security men had thrown her out and locked up.

I thought that would have put some sense into her head but it didn't. For the next two days, as soon as we got home, Amarkai would change, pick up the box with the sick kitten, and walk to the veterinary clinic. On the third day, when she wasn't home by 7:30 p.m., I couldn't cover for her anymore. I told Amerley-mami where she was. We waited until 8 p.m., and when she didn't come home, Amerley-mami and I walked to La.

On the way, Amerley-mami kept cursing her luck. How could she have such stupid daughters? How could she have a daughter who cared more about a cat than her own welfare? How could I, who was the oldest and was supposed to have more sense, have known where she was going and kept quiet? She said if anything happened to Amarkai it would be *on my head*. I prayed and prayed to God that my sister would be well and promised that I wouldn't be so stupid the next time. I'd take better care of all my sisters.

The veterinary clinic was closed when we got there. We were about to leave when we saw a security guard patrolling the yard. Amerley-mami asked if he had seen a girl with a kitten in a Key Soap box. The man asked us to follow him to the back of the building. He told us one of the vets, Dr. Lutterodt, had taken pity on her and the kitten and agreed to do the operation for free after working hours. Amarkai had begged to watch, so he had allowed her to assist him.

We entered through the back door and went to a room marked *Operating Room*. Amarkai, whom I had given up all hopes of finding alive, was still in her school uniform. She had a green face mask and wore goggles over her eyes and gloves on her hands. She was assisting a white-haired man who was operating on Vashti's kitten. Amarkai was in charge of pumping an inflatable ball connected to a mask over the kitten's face. She waved when she saw us. I saw the blood on her gloves and grew dizzy.

Neither Amerley-mami nor I could stand the sight of the blood, so we waited in the dark reception area. Amarkai's eyes were shining when she came out to join us after the procedure.

Though she knew she would get beaten that night, nothing could steal her joy—not even the murderous glances Amerley-mami kept throwing her way. Dr. Lutterodt called Amerley-mami to his office, where they spoke for a long time. When she came out later, something about her demeanor had changed. The three of us walked to the bus station and got a *trotro* that was going to Teshie. Amarkai fell asleep on the bus. Amerley-mami was lost in thought. That night she didn't whip Amarkai as I thought she would. She didn't whip her the next day either. Instead, on the third day, she told her Dr. Lutterodt had offered to sponsor her education and wanted her transferred from our school at Teshie to a private school at La. As her punishment, she would spend her weekends cleaning the clinic. Amarkai was delirious with joy.

Vashti was over the moon when her kitten came back two weeks later and started drinking milk from both the eyedrop bottle and its mother's teats. And I, I wondered how something so insignificant as helping a little girl's kitten could change your life forever.

CHAPTER 5

A minute before my life changed forever for the first time, I was kneeling in the cooking area with my face on the ground and my butt in the air. The side of my face lay flat on the smooth earth, and my cheeks were full of air as I blew my lungs out onto the damp wood between the three red clay mounds of our tripod stove.

Our cooking area was a shed made up of a thatched roof propped on four thick branches behind our building. Others cooked on their verandas on either gas or kerosene stoves, which we didn't have. Instead, we erected the shed behind the building and built the clay tripod stove. We put firewood between the clay mounds and balanced our pots on the tripod. It was almost as good as a coal pot. The only problem was that the firewood produced a lot of smoke.

"Whoo." I blew another lungful of air onto the logs, but instead of them catching fire, the newspaper I had lit between them smoldered and the flame died. Clouds of black smoke flowed into my eyes. I sat back and coughed. It looked like my sisters and I would have to make do with *kenkey* and *shitɔ* six days in a row.

It was already the middle of April and I knew Nuumo was just waiting for the last day of the month to come pounding on our door. Amorkor and Tsotsoo had been sent home two weeks earlier for not paying their school fees. Amarkai was the only one who kept going to school. Amorkor had forgotten to collect driftwood the day before. Instead of going to the beach behind our compound house for the driftwood, as I had asked, she had walked four miles to the library to return a book and borrow a new one. On her way back it had started to rain; she had forgotten all about the wood and rushed home with her book—*The Prison Graduate* by Efo Kodjo Mawugbe—tucked, snug and dry, underneath her blouse. Any other person would have been miserable that she was the main reason her family had had to eat *kenkey* and *shitɔ* for the fifth time that week, but Amorkor is not any other person. After she had eaten her ball of *kenkey* with *shitɔ*, she disappeared into the room and began reading her book. My sisters did not really mind that we were going to have *kenkey*. Our diet rarely varied. It was either *kenkey*, *gari*, or *banku*, and fried fish on the days when Nikoi gave me more than two cedis so we could eat a decent meal. Amerley-mami did not notice whether we had eaten or not, though I noticed that the portion of food we left for her every night was eaten by morning.

I would, however, give credit where credit was due, and before

I even got off my mattress that morning, Amorkor had been to the beach and back: driftwood was stacked by one of the walls in our cooking area. The only problem was that the driftwood was damp. I'm sure Amorkor had made the effort because she felt bad about the names Ofoe-mami, the *kenkey* seller, had called us before giving us the four balls of *kenkey* and six tablespoons of *shitɔ* on credit. By my calculations, we owed her fourteen cedis and fifty pesewas. Ofoe-mami's tongue is sharper than a scorpion's sting, but I didn't let her insults hurt me. They'd rolled off my skin like water off the feathers of a duck. Last night she had ranted and raved as usual.

"I'm not *Papa Bronya*! Do I look like Father Christmas? I also have children to feed! How can I feed them if I have to give away everything I make for free? Where is your mother? Is she not a woman like me? Why can't she cook for her children? And you, are you not grown enough to cook for your sisters? Are you not a woman?"

I had stood looking at my feet while Ofoe-mami rained insults on my mother, my father, my grandparents, my sisters, and finally on me. I hadn't dared look her in the face for fear she'd think I was being defiant or disrespectful. Afterward, when she had ranted and raved to her satisfaction and within hearing of all our neighbors, she had walked to the table. The *kenkey* was kept in a basin in a thick transparent plastic sheet to keep it hot. She drew the basin toward her, opened the sheet, dipped her hand into a bowl of water by her side, and picked out four balls of steaming fermented corn dough wrapped in corn leaves, one after the other. My stomach had rumbled. I had only had *gari* soakings to eat the whole day and I was hungry. She had placed the balls of *kenkey* in a black plastic bag and retied the knot on the sheet over the *kenkey*.

She had moved over to the wooden platter on which crisp fried shrimps and fish had been stacked like towering pyramids. I began to salivate and my stomach rumbled once more. Ofoe-mami took a smaller plastic bag and opened it and the bucket of *shitɔ* by her side. I had watched as she scooped two tablespoons of the spicy black pepper sauce into the bag, added four tablespoons of ground red pepper with tomatoes and onions, and deftly tied it. She placed it on top of the *kenkey* in the black plastic bag and dropped it into my waiting hands.

I had been about to ask if we could have some fish as well, but I'd seen the look on her face, and anyway, I had been insulted enough for one night. *One day,* I had sworn to myself, *one day I'll buy* kenkey *with enough fish and shrimps and I won't even eat the heads or tails.*

As if that had not been enough, on my way home Nuumo, our landlord, had met me at the gate.

"Tell your mother if I don't get the rent by the end of this month, you'll have to leave."

He didn't even wait for me to make my usual excuse of how she was sick and not feeling well. He just stormed off.

"Whoo." I blew on the logs again. Nothing happened.

"Sister Amerley! Sister Amerley! A car has stopped in front of our house. It's posh! When the door opened, cold air like the Harmattan wind came out, and the woman inside must be Miss Ghana or something." Tsotsoo said all this without pausing for breath. One hand covered her mouth.

I turned and looked around the cooking area. "Where's the lizard?"

She pointed to the rafters. I looked up and saw an extra large gray, black, and blue lizard with a red and orange crest sunning itself on one of the planks. I picked up a stone, aimed, and threw it. The lizard ran a few steps and then stopped to bob its head up and down. I shook my head; nothing I could say would make Tsotsoo remove her hand from her mouth. Her two upper front teeth had fallen out one after the other two weeks ago. Her playmates had told her that if a lizard saw the space where the teeth had been while she was talking, the new teeth would never erupt. Since lizards were a common sight on the walls and roofs of our house, Tsotsoo's hands were now permanently glued to her mouth.

"Sister Amerley, come and see!" Tsotsoo insisted, pulling me to my feet with her free hand.

Amarkai hurried into the cooking area. "The woman wants to see Amerley-mami."

"Sister Amerley, won't you go and greet the woman in the car?" Tsotsoo asked with her hand still over her mouth.

Vashti's cat came into the cooking area and rubbed its body around Amarkai's legs.

"Sister Amerley, if you don't go she'll think we're disrespectful," Amarkai said.

I looked from one sister to another. I wasn't going to fall for their prank. They'd been trying to trick me into going to see Amerley-mami the entire morning.

"Oh really," I said, pouring some kerosene from a green beer bottle onto the damp wood. "Tell her Amerley-mami is asleep."

"We already did. She said we should wake her up," Amarkai said, and from the look on her face I could tell she was serious.

I struck a match against the box and held it to the damp wood, knowing even as I did so that I was wasting both my time and the wood's.

"If this is a prank, we'll all eat *kenkey* this evening. I won't even try lighting this wood anymore, and I'll send both of you to get the *kenkey* from Ofoe-mami."

"Sister Amerley, we're not lying to you. Just come and see her," Tsotsoo said, dragging me out with one hand.

I followed Amarkai and Tsotsoo, though I expected them to start laughing about how I had fallen for their prank when we got to the main compound. To my surprise, there was indeed a black Jeep parked under the cashew tree. I could see movement behind our neighbors' curtains as people spied on us. I didn't blame them. I would have done the same if the situation had been reversed. This being a Sunday, almost everyone was home. But there would be no gossip tonight because there was no way the occupants of that car knew any of my family members. The car looked like it had just been oiled with shea butter. It gleamed and sparkled in the sunlight. A woman dressed in a rich green and gold lace *kaba* and *slit* stood by the back door. I could see why Tsotsoo thought she was Miss Ghana—she was beautiful. She was even more beautiful than the current Miss Ghana, and she was here to see Amerley-mami? Surely there must have been a mistake. This woman must have gotten our Amerley-mami mixed up with some other Amerley-mami. There was no way my mother knew someone this posh.

The woman had "fancy" written all over her. She had gold jewelry on her neck, ears, wrists, and fingers. Huge sunglasses hid her eyes and almost half of her face. When she used a hand to position her sunglasses properly, the gold bracelets on her wrists sparkled. I could see she felt uncomfortable as our neighbors came out of their rooms to stare at her. No longer satisfied with spying from behind their windows, all of the adults suddenly found reasons to be outdoors. The children openly gawked. Most of the older kids carried their younger brothers and sisters on their backs. I could count four children with runny noses, including Tsotsoo;

two others had conjunctivitis. They had been rubbing their red eyes the entire day.

I walked quickly to where she stood. Amarkai and Tsotsoo were close on my heels, their curious eyes fixed on the woman.

"Good afternoon, madam," I said.

"Oh hello, you must be Naa Amerley."

I gasped. How did she know that? A part of me was thinking, if she knew my name, that meant I also knew someone posh. I couldn't quite process that at the moment.

"Yes, madam," I stammered.

So she really did know my mother. How? Were they classmates? I very much doubted that since Amerley-mami had dropped out of school when she was ten. How did they know each other? A ripple of excitement went through me as I noted everything about her. I'd have a lot to tell Sheba when I saw her next.

"My! Look how you've grown," the woman said, taking a step toward me and reaching out as if she wanted to hug me. At the last minute she withdrew her hands and looked at me from head to toe, but not before I had caught a whiff of her perfume. She smelled like jasmine and orange blossoms. As she put her arms back by her side, I realized how dirty my sisters and I looked. We had not had a bath in four days. The taps had gone off a week ago, even at the church down the street. Though we had a drum full of water, we had begun rationing our supply, and bathing daily didn't feature high on our list of priorities.

"I'm Rosina, your mother's friend. Tell her I'm here."

Your mother's friend kept playing through my mind as I hurried to do as I was told. So Amerley-mami *did* know posh people. If Amerley-mami knew this woman, were there others we didn't know about? Amerley-mami had never mentioned a friend called Rosina. I hadn't even known Amerley-mami knew anyone who owned a private car. I didn't remember ever meeting this Rosina woman. There was no way I'd have forgotten her face, her clothes, or her smell.

It was a bad time to notice Amarkai hadn't swept in front of our room. Goat droppings lay scattered everywhere. I wiped my feet on the shabby welcome mat. Out of the seven letters only three remained—E, L, and M. Various mismatched *charley-wotes* lay scattered on and around the mat. I kicked them to the corner of the veranda and opened the screen door with the torn mosquito netting. I quickly rolled up our mattresses. I swept aside the faded curtain to Amerley-mami's sleeping area, where she lay on the bed. I nudged her, she groaned and asked me to go away, but I persisted.

"There's a woman here to see you. A posh woman. She's called Auntie Rosina."

Amerley-mami woke up instantly and sat upright. "Rosina?"

I nodded.

"Here?"

Another nod.

"Are you sure?"

Third nod.

She got out of bed and quickly changed out of her faded nightgown into an equally faded blue and purple tie-dyed *boubou*. She rinsed her mouth with a cup of water that was on a table by the bedside and spat the contents into the chamberpot we kept under the bed. Last night's urine was still in it. I didn't think now was a good time to go and empty it into the gutter in front of our house. She spread some Maxam toothpaste onto her finger and smeared it around her teeth and tongue and rinsed her mouth again. She washed her face, tried to comb her hair, but she hadn't retouched it in months so the comb couldn't run through it. She gave up and tied a scarf around it instead.

"What are you still doing here? Go and ask her to come in!"

I went outside to Auntie Rosina, who was still by the car.

Amarkai and Tsotsoo had joined some of the other kids and were gawking from underneath a nearby neem tree.

"Please, she says you can come in."

Auntie Rosina followed me into our room, and I stood watching in shock as she and Amerley-mami embraced.

Though I wanted to stay, I knew Amerley-mami would ask me to leave. In our neighborhood, children were to be seen and not heard. We were only to speak when we were spoken to. Aunty Rosina had come to visit Amerley-mami, so I was not needed. I went outside, where all the children gathered around me wanting to know who Auntie Rosina was, where she was from, what she wanted. I shooed them all away and went back to our cooking area.

My three sisters followed me there. Amorkor, who had disappeared somewhere so she could read her book in peace, reappeared.

"Is it true?" she asked me. "Tsotsoo says Miss Ghana is talking to Amerley-mami."

"She's not Miss Ghana," I said, because if Amorkor knew her books and Amarkai knew her animals, I could confidently say I knew my beauty queens. I could recite the names of the winners and runners-up of all the beauty pageants in Ghana for the past six years. I could even describe all the outfits they had worn. I have an excellent memory for details like that. Kofi-papa, our neighbor, bought his TV set six years ago. That was when I began watching the beauty pageants. At night he brought it out of his room onto his veranda and we all gathered at the feet of the adults to watch whatever was showing. Miss Malaika, Miss Ghana, Ghana's Most Beautiful, Miss Excel Plus—you name them, I knew them. I also knew Auntie Rosina hadn't participated in anything. Besides, she looked to be in her late forties.

"Take some water to her," I said to Amorkor, "but wash your hands first and be careful with the glass."

As Amorkor got up, I remembered she was the one who had broken three out of the six drinking glasses we had had. Amarkai had broken one and Tsotsoo had broken another.

"Never mind, I'll do it myself." I took out the last glass. There was a small chip on the rim. I hoped Auntie Rosina wouldn't notice.

"How about the driver?" Amarkai asked.

I looked through the plastic bowl we kept our dishware in. There were three stainless steel cups, four plastic cups, and two enamel cups. The stainless steel cups were all blackened, the plastic cups were just not presentable to an adult, and the enamel cups had chipped in various places and rusted metal showed through in others. I chose the one that had the fewest chips, filled it with water from the clay water-cooler, placed it on a plate, and handed it to Amarkai.

"Take it to the driver," I said.

I filled the glass with water, placed it on a second plate, and went back to our room. Amerley-mami and Auntie Rosina were seated side by side on the sofa. Amerley-mami's eyes were as red as ripe tomatoes. Tears flowed down her cheeks like a tap that had been turned on. Auntie Rosina looked distraught. I went up to her, offered the glass of water, and caught another whiff of the jasmine and orange blossom fragrance.

"Oh, you shouldn't have," she said, but she took the glass. Her fingernails were long and painted a deep red. Just as she was about to put the glass to her lips, she saw the chip and turned it away from her. She put the unchipped side to her lips and took a small sip. When she put the glass back down on the tray, there was a bright red lipstick mark on it. I could have stood there watching her all day but I was brought up better than that, so I turned and left.

Outside, my sisters and some of the neighborhood kids had surrounded the car and were making funny faces at their reflections. The tires of the car almost came up to Tsotsoo's shoulders. I went to join them. It was only then that I noticed I had sand from our kitchen floor on my left cheek and in my hair. No wonder Auntie Rosina hadn't wanted to hug me. I looked like a street child. In fact, all the children around me looked like street children. Most were barefoot. The boys wore shorts and the girls oversized blouses or T-shirts; most of the toddlers were naked. The few who were clothed wore only cotton underwear.

The driver was on the other side of the car wiping it with a duster. He looked quite young. I was guessing he was probably a few years older than Nikoi, who was nineteen. When he saw the children making funny faces and touching his shiny black car, he didn't chase them away like Bro Laryea does.

Bro Laryea drives a taxi and it's not even his, but he treats the car like it's alive and has feelings. He used to be a *trotro* driver and was Nikoi's former boss until he got the taxi. Every Sunday morning, rain or shine, he buys a packet of Omo powder and washes the car. Then he spends an hour polishing the dashboard and mirrors. You'd have thought the president or someone important was going to sit in it. He never gives any of us lifts.

Never. Not even when it's raining and the car is empty and he's going in our direction.

Auntie Rosina's driver reached for something in his car and came out with a bag of toffees. He gave one to each of us, including the neighborhood children. Many of the children checked to see if their sweet was the same size as the others'. The driver was lucky there, for if the sweets had been of different sizes, there would have been chants of: *Woasisi me. Me ne panin* or *Ofaine miji onukpa* and so on. When it came to the sharing of sweets and other goodies, the older children in the house were always quick to point out that since they were older they deserved a bigger share. Unfortunately, the same could not be said when it came to household chores. I was given a toffee. It had some red goo in it that stuck to the roof of my mouth and the backs of my teeth, but I loved the taste. It was a cross between *alasa* and mango.

Auntie Rosina and Amerley-mami came out. Amerley-mami called my siblings and me. As she stood beside Auntie Rosina, I saw how old she looked. She looked like she was Auntie Rosina's grandmother. They looked nothing like age-mates. She introduced each of us in turn. It must have been my imagination but I thought Auntie Rosina's gaze lingered on me longer than on my sisters. Tsotsoo went to stand by Amerley-mami's side and hid her face when it was her turn to be introduced. She had suddenly been overcome with shyness.

"So I'll come for her . . . I'll come back over the weekend," Auntie Rosina said.

The driver opened the door for her and she took out a large purse. A draft of cold air blew onto those of us standing by the car.

"Sorry I didn't bring you anything. Amerley, buy your sisters some toffees, okay?" She peeled off three five-cedi notes from a bundle and gave them to me. My eyes opened so wide I thought they'd fall out of their sockets. Fifteen cedis to buy toffees with?

"Oh no, auntie, it's okay," I said, though my fingers were itching to snatch the money from her hands. It was good manners to refuse money when it was first offered to you. Only after the person offered it a second or third time was it acceptable to collect the money.

"Oh come on. Get some ice cream or something. I promise, next time I'll shop for you. Here, take it."

I looked at Amerley-mami, who nodded her head, and I accepted the money. I turned to give it to her but Auntie Rosina stopped me. "No, that's for you and the girls."

She gave the rest of the wad to Amerley-mami, who went through the same refusing-the-money routine as I had before finally accepting it and tucking it into her bra. Auntie Rosina sat in her car, which was as cold as the deep freezer in the cold store down the road, and waved at us one more time before the driver took off. My sisters and I followed Amerley-mami to our room.

Amerley-mami bolted the door behind her, pulled the curtains down over the windows, took out the bundle of money, licked a finger, and quickly counted it. I counted alongside her but got mixed up when she went above one hundred. Amerley-mami was still counting the money when we heard a knock at the door. She quickly hid the money under her mattress.

"Amerley-mami? Amerley-mami?" It was our landlord. He had no doubt heard about our posh visitor and the money that had changed hands. There were a lot of "okro mouths" in our compound. In our neighborhood, gossip spread faster than the wind.

Amerley-mami took out the bundle, counted out forty of the notes, and stuffed them into my hands.

"Give this to him. Tell him I don't feel well."

I went out to give the money to Nuumo, who counted it quickly and left. I was glad to see him go, and so relieved that we wouldn't have to worry about rent for another year and nine months. When I got back inside, Amerley-mami had counted a few more bills and given them to Amorkor.

"Tomorrow, you and Tsotsoo will go to school. Go and give this money to Teacher Mensah. Tell him to pay your fees for you tomorrow. Go now before other people come to collect what I owe them."

Amarkai and Amorkor left the room together. Teacher Mensah lived in Madam Fosua's neighborhood. He was the assistant headmaster of their school. As my sisters left, I realized the cloud of fear and heaviness that had hovered over me since January was gone. It had completely lifted.

She looked at me. "What are we having for supper?"

I tried to hide my disappointment. I'd been expecting Amerley-mami to settle the cost of the apprenticeship with the seamstress so that I could start as well. She still had a lot of money in her hands.

"What are we having for supper?" she repeated.

She hadn't asked about our food ever since Ataa left. Maybe she'd go and see the madam and pay the bill herself.

"*Kenkey.*"

She made a face and asked, "How much do we owe Ofoe-mami?"

I told her the amount.

She handed me a twenty-cedi note. "Go and pay that bush woman before she comes knocking on our door. Add the change to what Auntie Rosina gave you. I feel like *domɛdo* and rice. Use whatever change is left to buy malt for you and your sisters."

Tsotsoo gasped and opened her mouth wide. For once she forgot to cover her mouth and I could see the pink gum where her front teeth had been. The area looked red. Her eyes were shining as she imagined herself drinking a whole bottle of Malta Guinness. In the past, the only times when bottles of Malta Guinness were opened in our house were when Amerley-mami and Ataa got important visitors and sent us to buy the drink for them. We only got to taste the drink if the visitors were kind enough to leave some of the dregs in the glasses.

"Can I have some *kelewele* too?" Tsotsoo asked with her mouth still uncovered.

"You can have anything you want," Amerley-mami said, smiling.

Despite not knowing the fate of my apprenticeship, I couldn't keep the smile off my face. I felt like Christmas had come in April as I practically ran to the night market. So this was how it felt to not have to worry about a thing. I felt lighter. I was sure if you had weighed me before Auntie Rosina showed up and if you weighed me now, there would be a significant difference. I felt like I was floating. I loved this feeling and I hoped it would last forever. Tsotsoo was on my heels, pulling up her shorts as she followed me. I made a mental note to buy an elastic band and sew it into her shorts. The smile on her face was one I would never forget. I'm sure even if she saw a hundred lizards she could not keep her mouth shut. She was practically glowing.

We made our way to the night market, which was what part of the *trotro* station became after sunset. In the evenings, people set up their wooden stalls in one corner of the station and sold all manner of foods straight from the fire. It was a pedestrian open-air market with space for one person at a time to walk between stalls. Kerosene lanterns and single electric bulbs provided the light.

Benches and plastic chairs and bowls of water for washing hands had been provided for customers. The air was filled with the smells of different foods. Music blared from speakers that had been set up in front of a stall that sold CDs and DVDs.

We waved at Sheba, who was selling pure water near the fried yam and *chofi* stall. Even though I could smell the fried turkey tails, I didn't look at the sieve with the meat arranged in it—it would only whet my appetite even more. The oil sizzled as the seller dropped pieces of peeled yam into the hot oil. We were not even deterred by the smells of fried eggs coming from the tea seller. I couldn't remember the last time I had eaten an egg. In addition to Milo tea and Lipton tea, she now also had moringa tea. We ignored the tantalizing whiffs of *banku* and okra soup when we passed by Daavi's stall. Though we could see crabs, *wele*, and chunks of meat floating in the soup, we walked on. Next to Daavi was her daughter, who was grilling big fat tilapias on a coal pot. Hawkers like Sheba walked between the stalls and sold everything from chewing gum to fruits to ice-cold drinks.

Ofoe-mami frowned when she saw me approaching. "As for this credit business, *dεε*, no wonder I'm not progressing! Do you people think I pluck leaves from trees to pay for the maize I buy from the market?"

I greeted her and paid her what we owed. She took the money, gave me my change, and stuffed the rest into her bra. A huge smile was on her face when she asked, "*Ei*, Amerley, is your father back?"

I shook my head.

"Then where—"

Before she could continue, a customer came to stand in front of the wooden tray on which she had piled her fried fish.

"Please, how much is this one?" the woman asked. She had tied a piece of cloth around her body. The straps of her bra showed above the cloth. She wore mismatched *charley-wotes* on her feet.

"Five cedis," Ofoe-mami said.

"*Ei*," the woman said, and walked away.

"*Bo dieŋtsɛ kwɛmɔ!* If you know you won't buy, why do you come and waste my time?" Ofoe-mami shouted after the woman's departing figure.

The woman turned and shouted, "Are you talking to me? When did it become a crime in this country to ask the price of something?"

Ofoe-mami tightened her own cloth around her waist and marched in the direction of the woman. I pulled Tsotsoo's hand. I didn't want us to be caught up in the fight. We made our way through the tightly packed stalls to the *domɛdo* and rice sellers. I bought boiled perfumed rice for each of us. She dished it out expertly into plastic bags. Then she ladled out the stew. She seemed disappointed when I said I wouldn't be buying any meat or fish to go with the rice. Tsotsoo and I practically ran to the *Pork-show* stall. The fat from the pork sizzled as it hit the charcoal beneath the grill. Black smoke rose up and bathed the meat. It was what

54

gave the meat its nice flavor. I ordered some and asked the seller to add more pepper when he turned the meat on the grill.

We joined a short line at the *kelewele* seller's stall. Eventually it was our turn and I bought some of the spiced fried plantains and fried groundnuts. I used the change to buy three bottles of ice-cold Malta Guinness.

CHAPTER 6

That night, after our feast of rice, *domɛdo*, and *kelewele* washed down with cups of Malta Guinness, Amerley-mami asked me to stay behind while my sisters went to watch *Efiewura* on Kofi-papa's TV set. She had been on her way to the bathroom. Amorkor had already put a bucket of water in the bathroom for her. I'd noted that the metal bucket needed scouring and had told Amorkor to do it the next day with pawpaw leaves, ash, and lime juice. She had grumbled but I knew she would do it. Amerley-mami had wrapped her cover cloth around her body. She held the pail we shared and her red sponge in one hand. In the other was the ball of *alata samina*, the local soap, we used for bathing.

"Tidy up the room," she said as she went out.

"Amerley-mami, I'll do it when I come back," I grumbled.

"Do it now and don't go anywhere. I want to talk to you."

While she took her bath, I tidied our room. I was certain she was going to talk to me about my apprenticeship, or she was going to give me a lecture about how I was to apply myself and learn all I could and not be lazy so as not to waste the money she was spending on me. I took my sisters' dirty clothes and stuffed them into the basin. We'd have to go and wash them at the beach tomorrow. I emptied the chamberpot into the gutter behind our house and swept out the ash from the mosquito coils.

There wasn't much I could do about the curtains. We washed them once a year at Christmastime, when we also scrubbed the mosquito nets. I was still grumbling when Amerley-mami walked in after her bath. She smelled fresh and nice. The lemony smell of the *alata samina* filled the room. She poured some Saturday Night powder into her hands and smeared it around her neck, between her breasts, and in her armpits.

"There's no need to grumble so much. I asked you to stay behind because I want to talk to you," she said as she handed me the threadbare towel we shared. I took the towel and added it to the dirty things in the basin.

I knew my mother well enough to know that she was not to be rushed. Whatever she had to say, she'd say it in her own good time. She removed the bedsheet from her bed and dumped it into the basin. I don't think it had been changed for six months. She looked in her suitcase and brought out the spare bedsheet. It had blue and white stripes and she only used it when Ataa was home. I looked at her in surprise.

"There are going to be some changes around here," she said as she tucked in the corners around the mattress. I went to the opposite side of the bed and tucked the sheet under the mattress. Afterward we straightened the corners until the blue and white stripes ran parallel to the headboard. She took a mosquito coil out of its box, placed it on the metal stand, and lit it.

"Come, sit by me," she said, indicating a space on the freshly made bed.

I looked down at the dirty clothes I was wearing, at the dirt on my body, and then at the neat bed.

"It's just a bedsheet. Come and sit."

I sat beside her.

"Rosina wants you to live with her and help her with her house chores."

My heart fell into my stomach. I looked down at the glowing red tip of the mosquito coil.

"I thought you'd be excited," Amerley-mami said.

I couldn't look at her. I felt tears sting my eyes.

"I thought you were going to talk to me about the apprenticeship. I thought you were going to give me the money to pay the madam."

"I'm coming to the good part," Amerley-mami said, taking my hand. "I told Rosina you want to be a seamstress. She's asked that you work for her for two years, and after that she'll enroll you in one of those big fashion schools. Isn't that fantastic? She told me those people sew clothes for all the big-shot women in this country. You'll learn so much more there than you could ever learn from this woman in her container store."

I didn't know how I felt. On the one hand I was thrilled at the prospect of going to a more prestigious fashion school, but on the other hand I was scared of leaving home. I had never been away from home before. Never. Not even for a night.

"So she wants me to be her maid?"

"No, no, not a maid. How can you say that? We're practically related, I've known her since we were children. Her grandmother's grandmother and Awo's grandmother were sisters-in-law. She's your aunt, besides; she's already got two house helps, so I don't think the work will be a lot."

"But—"

"Look, I will not lie to you. I don't have anything to give to you and your sisters. And your father . . . only God knows where he is. This is your chance to leave this place and make something of yourself."

I continued watching the glowing tip of the mosquito coil as a thousand and one thoughts ran through my head. What my mother was saying was true. All my life I've wanted to be a seamstress. Yesterday, when I had gone to Ofoe-mami to buy *kenkey* on credit, one mannequin in the local madam's container shop had been in a *kaba* that had lace sleeves and frills around the neck. I recognized the style. It was something Akushika Acquaye had worn two weeks ago while she reported the news. The second mannequin was in a pink caftan. White shiny thread had been used for the embroidery. It was very pretty.

"She just wants to help us," Amerley-mami said.

"Then why can't she pay for me to be an apprentice here, like what Dr. Lutterodt does for Amarkai? Why do I have to work for her for two years?"

"She's agreed to pay Amarkai and Tsotsoo's school fees for the next two years and to give me some money to trade with in exchange for your services."

I started to cry. How could she even agree to something like that without asking me? How could they have settled everything between themselves, as if I were a goat being traded at the market? Why couldn't she have even asked me if I wanted to go? I wasn't afraid of the work. I could cook, clean, sweep, wash, scrub, and weed in my sleep. But I was afraid that everything I wanted for myself would disappear if I agreed to become Auntie Rosina's maid. Would Amerley-mami be happy with Amorkor and Tsotsoo's fees being paid for just two years? What if they later decided between themselves that I'd work for Auntie Rosina for the duration of Amorkor and Tsotsoo's schooling? What if Auntie Rosina decided she didn't want to send me to the fashion design school anymore? The more I thought of these things, the harder I cried. The lightness I had felt earlier that evening was long gone. The heaviness was back. I know she hadn't done anything to warrant my distrust, but I didn't trust Auntie Rosina. I trusted my mother even less.

"Look at me, Amerley, look at me. I'm not working, where am I going to get the money to keep paying the rent, to keep feeding and clothing you and your sisters? If Rosina hadn't come today, we'd have been out on the streets by the end of the month. As for that father of yours, *dɛ*, the least said about him, the better!"

I cried even harder.

Amerley-mami was getting angry. "Amerley, why are you so ungrateful? Do you know how many girls would gladly exchange positions with you? Do you know what opportunities you'll be getting? This is your chance to do something with yourself and you sit here crying! Do you want to end up like me? There's nothing here for you—nothing for you and your sisters. If you don't get out now, the next thing is that you'll get pregnant, or do you think I don't know about you and Nikoi? Do you want to end up like Sheba?"

I took offense at that. Due to the *dumsor dumsor* situation with the electricity, Sheba's pure water business was not doing too well. Power supply was erratic and all those in the frozen food sector complained. But in the last few months, Sheba had helped feed my sisters and me while my mother had lain in bed. The only reason why I wasn't doing the same thing as Sheba was that I knew she'd eventually end up like my mother, depending on her man for her daily sustenance. I wanted more than that for myself. Way more than that. And Nikoi? How dare she judge Nikoi? Did she not know what he had done for us?

"Don't talk that way about Nikoi. He paid our rent and he's saving to buy me a sewing machine," I said, my confusion and disappointment giving way to anger.

"They say, 'If a naked man says he'll give you clothes, you should ask him what his name is.'"

I rolled my eyes. I didn't think now was the time for her to be telling me local proverbs.

"But Amerley-mami, it's true. If it hadn't been for the money he gave us, Nuumo would have kicked us out in January."

"If he has money to spend, he should look after his family."

It was true that Nikoi's family was no better off than ours, but that didn't give Amerley-mami the right to talk about him that way. Nikoi might not have met her criteria for a suitable boyfriend for me, but she lost her right to complain when she stopped being a responsible parent. Nikoi was an honest man, he worked hard as a driver's *mate*, and if it hadn't been for him, we'd have been sleeping on Sheba's veranda.

"The way you have looked after us these past months? He's been giving me money to feed us while you've lain in bed pretending to be sick."

The next thing I knew there was a throbbing pain on the left side of my cheek and I was sprawled flat on Amerley-mami's bed. I hadn't even seen her raise a hand. I tasted blood in my mouth and I wasn't sure where it came from. Either my cheek or my tongue.

She was furious. Her breath came out in spurts and her nostrils were flaring.

"You think you can insult me because of those dirty one-Ghana notes he gives you, *eh*? And what do you give him in return? He's buying you a sewing machine and giving you a few measly notes in exchange for what? Your body? Have you become an *ashawo*?"

I held my palm to my cheek and said nothing as the tears streamed down my face.

"Oww!" The shouts of disappointment rose as one from outside our room as we were all plunged into pitch darkness. The blackouts were almost as frequent as the water shortages. We shouldn't have been surprised by it, but we still shouted whenever the lights went out.

"Wipe your tears before your sisters come back, and prepare to leave on Saturday," Amerley-mami said as she struck a match to light a candle.

I knew this was the last time we would be discussing this. My mother had found a way to make money for herself, to be independent from her husband, and she wasn't about to give it up. I was her one-way ticket out of poverty. I pushed aside the furniture in the living room and rolled out the mattresses. I lay down and pretended to sleep as my sisters walked in, but my mind was spinning. If I didn't accept Auntie Rosina's offer, it wouldn't be long before we were back where we had started—struggling for rent money, school fees, and money for our basic upkeep. What if Auntie Rosina was trustworthy? What if she stuck to her word and enrolled me in that fashion design school? Was I on the verge of throwing away a golden opportunity? Did I want to spend the rest of my life being responsible for my sisters?

"As for the electricity company, *paa*, they wait until we're watching *Efiewura* before they know they have to take away the power," Amarkai said, changing into an undershirt. Later in the night it would become too hot to wear our cotton nighties.

I heard Amerley-mami's bed creak as Amarkai and Tsotsoo climbed into the bed.

"Amerley-mami, can I use the candle?" Amorkor asked.

"Are you going to read in this darkness? You'll spoil your eyes. Go to sleep," Amerley-mami said as she propped open the windows with a plank of wood.

Amerley-mami pulled down the mosquito net and tucked it around her mattress. She lit another mosquito coil and placed it between Amorkor's mattress and mine. She blew out the candle and climbed in beside Amarkai and Tsotsoo.

Amorkor, lying beside me, pulled her cloth over her head and pretended to sleep as well.

I lay listening to the night sounds as one by one my family fell asleep. Tsotsoo was the first to go. Then Amarkai. Then

Amerley-mami. When Amorkor was sure my mother was asleep, she climbed out of her bed, groped for the candle in the dark, and struck a match.

She pulled out her book and began to read while cupping the flame with one hand. I was looking the other way and watched as the flickering flames threw dark shadows on the wall. About an hour later, she blew out the candle, covered her head with her cloth, and fell asleep in minutes.

I couldn't sleep, and it wasn't just because of the stifling heat. The open window barely let in any air. There was another building directly in front of it, and it blocked the breeze coming from the sea. Tsotsoo mumbled in her sleep and flung an arm over Amarkai. Amorkor swiped at a mosquito and rolled over.

I got up. Though it was pitch dark, I knew my way around. My mattress was right by one of the armchairs. I held on to it as I got out of bed and felt my way toward the rough surface of the center table. From there it was three toe-to-heel steps to the front door. I put my hand out and lowered it to hip level, where my fingers traveled along its length until I felt the handle and the lock. Fraction by fraction, I turned the key in the lock and eased the door open. The difference in temperature was marked. The cool air breeze dried out the beads of sweat on my body.

The compound was silent. Some of the older children from the surrounding rooms had spread mats under the cashew and neem trees and were fast asleep. One of the landlord's dogs raised his head as I came out of the room. When he realized it was me and not Amarkai, his tail drooped and he went back to sleep. I slipped out of the compound and walked past the cooking area, where another dog had her nose in one of the baskets that held our utensils. I shooed her away. Even if I left her, she wouldn't find anything there apart from *gari*.

I could hear the waves even before I got to the sea. I chose the path that would keep me away from the rocks. I walked past the stretch of beach where the fishermen kept their canoes and to an abandoned shack where some of the men in the area were living. I wondered if Nikoi was asleep or if he had gone out with his friends. A light flickered in the shed. I crept toward the open door and looked in.

Inside, hip-life music played from someone's phone. A kerosene lantern sat on an upturned carton. It cast a dull glow on the room, and thick black smoke billowed from it. I doubted if anyone trimmed the wicks. Some people were asleep on mats. Girls lay entwined in the arms of their boyfriends. Two boys were huddled in a corner sharing a cigarette and arguing about a soccer match. Around their feet were chewed sticks of sugarcane. The room smelled of stale sweat, cheap beer, and cigarette smoke.

"*Ei*, Amerley, come in and greet us," one of the boys called out. He was in an undershirt and a pair of shorts. A dirty bandage was tied around his left knee. Even from where I stood by the door I could see the gap where a front tooth had once been. The tooth next to it had turned brown.

I tiptoed through the tangled mass of bodies and sometimes had to step over people as I went closer to where they sat.

"Good evening, Tsina," I said, and shook his hand. I didn't know the other guy's name. I nodded in his direction. He nodded back. Tsina was Sheba's on-again, off-again boyfriend. He was also the father of her unborn baby. They were in their off phase. Tsina had always wanted to be a boxer and he used to train really hard at it. When he was sixteen he had entered a juvenile boxing competition at Bukom. Unfortunately for him, he had been knocked out in the third round by a fifteen-year-old. It was in that same fight that his front tooth had been knocked out. Sometimes when he laughed and threw his head back I could see bits of the broken root in the gum. Sometimes the gum around it got swollen and dirty water came out.

A knee injury, the result of falling out of the ring in another fight, put an end to his boxing ambitions. Now he was a truck pusher if there was no other work to be done.

"*Ei, lai momo.* So if I don't ask of you, you won't ask of me, *eh?*"

I smiled. "I'm busy. You know my mother is not well."

"Busy for the where? But you always make time for Nikoi."

I smiled again. "Where is he?" Just hearing his name made my heart beat faster.

Tsina shrugged. "Where else?"

I thanked him and left the shack.

I loved the beach at night. I loved the serenity and calmness I felt when I walked there, and I loved that there were fewer people there. As I got closer to the grove of coconut trees, I could hear the gentle strumming of a guitar. My feet quickened of their own accord. I could make out the silhouette of a person sitting at the foot of one of the trees. A lit stick of cigarette was at his lips.

I slid down the tree and sat next to him. I pulled the cigarette out of his mouth and ground it into the sand. I didn't fancy dying of lung cancer from cigarettes I didn't even smoke. I settled my head on his shoulder, and all the anguish I'd been feeling in my heart floated away with the notes he played. He played for a few more minutes before placing the guitar aside and pulling me close to him.

"I thought you weren't coming," he said.

"I couldn't get away."

I wound the gold chain he wore around his neck on my finger.

"But the lights went off hours ago."

"Amorkor was reading."

"*Ei*, that's your 'book-long' sister! I'm sure if she had her way we'd have twenty-three hours of daytime and only one hour of darkness so she can read all day long."

I smiled and snuggled closer into his side.

"I heard you got a very important visitor today."

I groaned. Was there anyone who hadn't heard about Auntie Rosina's visit?

"She's related to my mother. Their great-grandmothers were in-laws or something like that."

"I didn't know you knew any important people."

"I didn't know she existed until today."

"I hear your mother has paid your rent and your sisters' fees in full."

I sighed. How many "okro mouths" were there in that compound house? I'm sure Auntie Rosina's visits provided fodder for all the gossips in the neighborhood.

"Yes."

Nikoi pushed me away from him. I looked down but he lifted my chin up and in the moonlight he stared into my eyes. He knew me well enough to know I was worried.

"Amerley, what's wrong?"

My throat felt sore and again I felt tears prick behind my eyes.

"Everything."

I buried my face in his shoulder and told him everything that had happened.

"You're leaving?"

"I don't have a choice!"

"We could run away."

"To where? Where would we go? I don't have any money and

I don't want to be a *kayayo*." Everyone knew that the life of head porters was tough.

We lay on the cold sand together. Nikoi stroked my arm absentmindedly. I could tell his thoughts were miles away, and I could almost hear the wheels in his head turn as he weighed the pros and cons of my options.

"Maybe it's not a bad thing," he said at last.

I looked at him through my tear-stained eyes. "What do you mean?"

"I mean don't they say every cloud has a silver lining? I think you should go."

"What? Are you crazy?"

"Amerley, look at it this way: you work for her for two years and she enrolls you in a prestigious fashion design school afterward, all expenses paid. It's far better than working with that too-known madam on the next street. She is proud and she behaves as if she knows everything and looks down on the rest of us."

"Nikoi, what's wrong with you?"

I shrugged his hand off my shoulder and jerked away from him when he tried to touch me.

"Amerley, it took me almost a year to save the money I gave you. When will we ever finish buying the things on that list? When will I save enough money to buy my own taxi? And come on, we both know that our madam doesn't know as much about sewing as she pretends to. She only specializes in *slit* and *kaba*. I've heard people say if you take designs out of a magazine or catalogue, she just spoils your material for you. Last month she had to refund the cost of a wedding gown to one of her customers. Do you really want to be like that, or do you want be an expert in all types of clothes—skirt suits, dresses, evening gowns, wedding gowns, whatever is in style?"

"I can't believe you're saying this."

He stroked my cheek. "I'm looking ahead, Amerley. If this woman takes you in, she pays your sisters' fees, they go to school, make something of themselves, and become independent. If you stay, they'll continue being your responsibility for the rest of our lives and we'll end up like our parents—barely making ends meet, living from hand to mouth each month, always worrying about bills and where our next meal is going to come from. I'm tired of living like that."

"I'm sorry you have to worry about me and my sisters. We're not your responsibility."

"Stop that foolish talk. You're my girl. If I don't look after you, who will? Besides, it's only for two years. By the time you're done, I should have my own taxi. It doesn't even matter if it's just a secondhand one. I'll work night and day to make sure we don't have to beg for anything."

"But what if Auntie doesn't do what she says? What if she does not enroll me in that fashion design school?"

"But what if she does?"

We were both quiet while I thought things through.

"She gave Amerley-mami money to start her own business."

"Yes. You already told me."

"Do you think Amerley-mami would run a good business?"

"Well, she had better. I don't think an opportunity like this will come her way again."

"Plus we paid the rent in full for the next one and a half years, so she won't have any major expenses for some time. I think if she puts her mind to it she can start earning some money."

Nikoi nodded while I sorted through my thoughts.

"This is what I'll do," I said finally. "I'll go to Auntie Rosina's for the two years. If she does enroll me in the school, then that's a bonus. If she doesn't, I'll just come back. You'll have saved enough for my apprenticeship with the madam here, right?"

"Right."

"And if Amerley-mami manages her business well, my sisters will not be my responsibility anymore. The only thing I'd have to think about would be us."

"Exactly," Nikoi said, drawing me in for a hug.

Though I'd spoken the words as if I had everything figured out, I was still scared. Just thinking about it made my heart beat faster and made me feel anxious. I wondered how I was going to survive two years without my sisters, without Sheba, and without Nikoi.

"I'll miss you," I whispered.

A shiver ran down my body but it had nothing to do with the weather.

Nikoi thought I was cold and pulled me closer to him, and the heat from his body warmed me up.

"I'll miss you too, but you'll still be in Accra. East Legon isn't in the Northern Region. It's just an hour's drive away."

"But I won't get to see you every night like this."

"I'll miss this—sitting and talking with you," he whispered as his hand snaked underneath my blouse.

Though my skin tingled and I felt electric shivers creep down my spine, I swatted his hand away.

He groaned. "Amerley, you're leaving on Saturday."

"I told you I'm not having sex until I get married."

"Yeah, I know." He sighed and pulled me back into his embrace.

"Will you wait for me?"

"What do you mean?" he asked.

"There are other girls who . . ."

He laughed. "I should be the one asking you that. You'll go to East Legon and see all those boys who have so much money they don't even know what to do with it. I should be the one worried that you won't want to come back."

"I will, I promise."

He kissed me. "I know you will, and I'll be waiting when you come back."

"Play something for me," I said, snuggling close to him.

He picked up his guitar and began strumming. I fell asleep in his arms listening to him play the chorus of Raquel's "Candyman." He woke me up just before dawn and walked me home. I crept back into our room and went back to sleep. I was no longer afraid of leaving. Everything would work out and Nikoi would still be waiting for me when I got back.

CHAPTER 7

Saturday morning dawned bright and clear. The previous day
I had gone with Amerley-mami to Makola Market to buy the
plastic cups and bowls she was going to sell. I still didn't know
exactly how much Auntie Rosina had given her, but she had
gone to the wholesalers and bought five hundred plastic cups
and bowls. I hadn't said a word to her since the night she slapped
me. It still hurt that she wouldn't use part of the money for my
apprenticeship. She had bought me three blouses, three skirts,
three dresses, one pair of dress shoes, one pair of sandals, and
a towel. They were all *fos*, but even though they had been used
before, they still looked new. She also bought five panties, three
brassieres, one sponge, and a pair of *charley-wotes*. Those were
brand new.

At home my sisters watched with envy as I packed the things
into a small secondhand suitcase. I had had my bath by the time
they woke up. Amerley-mami had gone out to buy them *koko* and
koose. Amorkor sneaked out to buy some more sugar. The sugar

75

was tied in sections in a long plastic bag. They looked like large rosary beads. Each of us got two of the tied bags.

"Sister Amerley, I can't believe you're going," Amarkai said, stroking one of the blouses.

"I'll come and visit."

"You're so lucky," Amorkor said, scrubbing her teeth with the *kotsa* she'd been chewing. "Just imagine, you might meet some rich guy and fall in love."

I snorted. "Those things only happen in books. Do you think rich guys want girls like us?"

"If you don't have faith, it won't happen to you. It's almost like a Cinderella story and Auntie Rosina is the fairy godmother. Now you just have to meet Prince Charming and fall in love and live happily ever after," Amorkor said, clapping her hands in delight.

I snorted even louder. I enjoyed a good story as much as anyone else, but I had the sense to know where fairy tales ended and the real world began. Amorkor read everything—books, scraps of newspapers that the sellers wrap fish in, inscriptions on T-shirts, labels on bottles . . . everything. She'd read the Bible cover to cover three times. Sometimes I thought her body needed words to live, the way the rest of us need water. If she didn't have anything to read, she became cranky. She owned eight books. She had received five from speech- and prize-giving day at school, got one as a birthday gift when Amerley-mami and Ataa were on better terms, had found one just lying there on the street, and had stolen one from the library. She had liked *The Jasmine Candle* so much she hid it under her blouse when no one was watching and walked out of the library.

I liked to read too, but practical things like newspapers, the Bible, textbooks, and recommended literature books like *The Blinkards* and *The Merchant of Venice*. I'd started reading both of them in senior high school, before I got sent home for not paying my fees. I hadn't finished reading either book, but the little I had read, I had enjoyed. While Amorkor read anything and everything, it was books about princes and princesses and silly stories like that she absolutely loved.

"Ah beg, tell me, who in their right minds would fall in love with a beast?" I asked.

Amarkai was giggling when she said, "Or speak to a mirror and stand there while it answers. *Ei*, that one is like *juju*, the way the *wulomei* look into a calabash of water and see things."

"*Oyiwa*, tell her. As for being a *mami wata* and coming on land, *dɛ*, don't even go there," I said, laughing.

"Well, if you put it that way, it does sound scary. It's true if someone came here and waved a wand and changed mice into horses and made my dress change into a glamorous gown, I wouldn't stand there and talk to her," Amorkor said.

"I tell you no lie, I'd probably run to a church and ask for deliverance or something. White people, don't they fear anything?

I mean, why would you kiss a dead body? And if the person came back to life, would you stand there and watch?" I asked, giggling.

"Sister Amerley, I'd run even faster than the wind," Tsotsoo said from behind her covered mouth.

"I prefer Ananse stories. There're no *tolis* in those ones," Amarkai said.

"But if a prince on a white horse came and said he wanted to marry you and he changed your life forever, wouldn't you like it?" Amorkor asked.

"Get your head out of the clouds and stop dreaming," I replied. "If anyone is going to change your life, it's you. No fairy godmother or Prince Charming or rich aunt or anyone else is going to do that. I'm glad Auntie Rosina is helping us, but she won't do it forever. You girls have to study hard when you go to school. Don't wait for anyone to change your lives for you. If you don't like the life you're living, change it yourself."

My sisters sat at my feet, and I sat on my suitcase.

"You, Amorkor, you love reading and that's good, but you've got to love your schoolwork as much as you love your storybooks. You've got your exams coming up soon. Amarkai, you're lucky Dr. Lutterodt is paying for you to go to a good school, so you really have to study hard next year when you start JHS. Tsotsoo, you're six and you still don't know your two times tables. If you don't learn, you won't become anything. Don't you all want to be 'big' women like Auntie Rosina and ride in posh cars?"

My sisters nodded.

"If I were as rich as Auntie Rosina, I'd have a library in my house, which would be bigger than our room, and I'd just spend every minute in there," Amorkor said.

"But Sister Amorkor, won't you come out and eat?" Tsotsoo asked, her eyes opening wide but her hands still over her mouth.

"No. I would only read and read and read. I wouldn't ever feel hungry."

Amarkai snorted. "You'd end up dead beside your books. If I were as rich as Auntie Rosina, I'd open a veterinary clinic for people who can't afford treatment for their animals."

I could see Amarkai doing just that—starving while she fed some mangy animal.

"If I were Auntie Rosina, I would eat cake and meat pies and drink malt every day. I wouldn't ever eat *gari* soakings or *kenkey* again," Tsotsoo said.

My sisters were still chattering when we heard a knock on our door. Nikoi peeped through the torn netting. Tsotsoo got up and ran to him. "Bro Nikoi!" She hugged his legs. He put his hand into his pocket and brought out five condensed milk toffees. Tsotsoo got two. The rest of us got one each.

I got off the suitcase and followed him out of the room. I didn't want Amerley-mami to come and meet him there. We walked hand in hand to the beach. On the way he cut a young branch off a neem tree, stripped off its bark, and began to clean his teeth. We didn't say anything. We didn't have to. Everything that needed saying had already been said. We walked past the line of canoes, past the ramshackle hut, and past the grove of coconut trees; we would have walked to the moon if we could have.

When we were out of sight of all the other people, Nikoi stopped and just stared at me. I had the feeling that he wasn't just memorizing the details of my face, he was looking deeper into my eyes—into my very soul. Despite the warmth of the air, I shivered.

He spat the stick out, cupped my face, and kissed me. Nikoi had kissed me many times before, but this—this was unlike anything I'd ever experienced. It was almost like he wanted to possess me, to enter my body, to become me.

When we pulled apart he slipped his hand into his pocket and brought out a ring. It wasn't like the ones they showed on the soap operas—the types with the huge diamond in the center that sparkled when it caught the sun's rays. Where would he have gotten the money to buy me a ring like that? The ring was white, carved out of some type of bone. I'd have liked to think it was ivory but I knew better. I'd seen thousands of them for sale by the side of the street.

"I know it's not much. It's only temporary. One day I'll get you the real thing. I promise. This won't be our life anymore."

I might not believe in fairy tales, but here was my very own Prince Charming, and I believed everything he said.

He took off the gold chain he wore around his neck. He slipped on the bone ring and clasped it around my neck. The ring lay in the hollow between my breasts. Nikoi didn't have to say anything for me to know how important that act was to him. I twirled the chain around my finger. I'd never worn gold before. I didn't know the right words to thank him, so I kissed him back instead and let it say everything that needed saying.

An hour later I got home to find Auntie Rosina's driver had been waiting for me. Amerley-mami's face was tight with anger but I didn't care. She pushed the plastic bag containing my porridge and bean cakes into my hands. The driver put my suitcase in the trunk. I hugged each of my sisters goodbye. All three of them were crying. Sheba and Vashti had also come to say bye. Amarkai's retinue of animals stood by her side, sniffing her hands, rubbing her legs, trying to get her attention.

Amerley-mami stuffed a ten-cedi note into my hand. "You'll not get another opportunity like this one. Don't mess it up."

I climbed into the front seat beside the driver. It was so cold I shivered. He rolled the windows down and turned the air conditioner off.

I didn't look back as we drove away. I was afraid I'd jump out of the car and run back home. When he drove on the beach road,

I swear I heard the strumming of a guitar above the roar of the ocean. It couldn't have been my imagination.

For most of the drive out of Teshie my mind wasn't on the scenery. My mind was in a thousand different places at once—at the beach with Nikoi, at the cooking area behind our house, in our one-room home, at the La Veterinary Center—everywhere but in the car.

The next thing I knew we were in East Legon. How was it possible to have lived all your life in a city and never seen the other side? The houses were larger than any I had ever seen. Their gates and walls were twice my height. Most had electric fences. There were hardly any people on the streets. Just lots of four-by-fours with tinted windows, which disappeared into the walled houses. There were no choked gutters, no *trotros* on the street, no hawkers or peddlers.

The driver pulled up in front of a gate. The gate slid open by itself. I took a deep breath as he drove into the compound. Day one of the next two years had begun.

CHAPTER 8

Auntie Rosina's compound was vast. I couldn't see the entire fence wall though I knew it was present. We could have fit the compound house in Teshie into it four times over. The grass on the lawn was greener than any I had ever seen. All types of flowers and plants grew around the well-cut lawn. Pink and orange hibiscus hedges and red ixora hedges lined the driveway to the front of the house. Flowerpots filled with roses, lilies, marigolds, orchids, and numerous green leafy plants were all over the compound. Beyond the gate, we drove for about three minutes before we got to the house itself. The house was huge. It was painted cream and brown. The windows and doors were all brown. Decorative bricks had been used in some places. Creeping plants—morning glory, passion fruit, and a vine with yellow flowers—grew on a trellis attached to one wall. More plants hung from balconies and ledges. We didn't stop in front of the massive wooden doors, though, but drove to the back, to the kitchen.

"Madam will see you when she wakes up," said the driver,

who had introduced himself as Nii Okai. It was the same driver who had brought her a week ago to Teshie. My eyes might have betrayed the surprise I felt. It was almost noon. Who slept until twelve in the afternoon?

"She gets migraines if she wakes up before twelve. A word of warning: Never, ever wake her up before twelve, not even if there's an earthquake or a tsunami. She'll never forgive you if you do. The last house help who did that got fired."

A knot formed in my stomach. She fired someone for waking her up before twelve? What sort of woman was this?

"I'll send your things to the servants' quarters. Go through that door to the kitchen. Magajia, she's the boss around here. She'll tell you what to do."

I nodded and walked up to the kitchen. I knocked on the door. I didn't get a response. I knocked again and waited. There was no sound coming from behind the door. I tried the handle. It wasn't locked. A blast of cold air hit me when I entered the room. I stood there amazed by its size. It was massive. It was four times the size of our room in Teshie. Sunlight streamed in from the open windows and played hopscotch on the walls. The countertops were all marble and they shone. Two fridges and one very long freezer hummed in their corners. The stove—I'd never seen a stove like that before—it gleamed. It looked like they had just had it delivered from a shop. On one of the burners was a pan of boiling palm fruits. There were two ovens on the wall. I hadn't seen anything like those either. The cupboards were so shiny you'd have thought they had just been sandpapered and lacquered. Everything was clean. There were no basins with utensils and cups or anything of that sort. No black cauldron filled with water to soften the burnt *banku* crust at the bottom.

A bowl of big red apples stood in the center of the table beside a vase of freshly cut sunflowers. The only apples I had ever eaten were the green ones. Usually we got two small apples for one cedi when they began to turn yellow and spoil. The only flowers I'd seen inside people's homes were the plastic ones, and usually those were faded and covered in so much dust that you couldn't even tell the colors.

An open door led away from the kitchen. I followed it to a hallway. I didn't understand how there could be so much space with nothing in it. No suitcases, no drums of water or water containers, no red and white or blue-and-white checked Ghana-must-go bags, nothing. Just a vast space with paintings on the walls. One of the paintings was of a bustling local market showing market mammies in their broad cane hats sitting behind their wares. Another was of the beach: a single canoe with the inscription *Jeee nyɛhe sane* was tied to a coconut tree. All the other paintings were of dogs— different breeds of dogs.

I heard a sound and followed it to a living room. A woman,

older than my mother but not as old as Awo, was arranging white lilies on a center table. There were plants growing in pots all over the room, ferns and other very leafy plants. The woman was in a shapeless black skirt and an oversized white shirt. Her hair was plaited with black thread. She wore no earrings or jewelry. On her feet were brown sandals.

Big cream leather chairs were arranged around the table. Various candles and figurines were on a shelf on one of the walls. On another wall was a painting of the back of a naked woman. A third wall had photos—a few of them were of Auntie Rosina and a man I assumed was her husband. Most of them were of children, charting their growth from when they were babies to what I was assumed were their current ages. There were two children—a boy and a girl. The boy looked to be the same age as me, sixteen. The girl looked younger, maybe twelve or thirteen. She looked younger than Amorkor but older than Amarkai.

"Good afternoon, auntie," I said.

The woman gave a small yelp of fright and turned in my direction.

"Who are you? How did you get in?"

"My name is Amerley. Auntie Rosina sent for me. Nii Okai said I could come in."

"Nii Okai said you could come in and so you just walked in. Don't you have the sense to see the floors are still wet? Look at the mess you've created!"

I turned to look at what she was pointing at. It was only then that I noticed the floors had just been mopped. I had left a track of dirty shoe prints leading from the corridor to the living room.

"Take that mop and clean it right this minute!"

I looked where she pointed. A mop and bucket lay there. I just stared at her.

"Ah ah? Are you deaf? Didn't you hear me? The floor won't mop itself, you know? Take that mop and get to work right this minute! And next time don't use the kitchen door. I don't want the likes of you hanging around my kitchen. Use the side door."

She left me standing there and walked out. I felt tears prick my eyes. I didn't even know why I wanted to cry. It certainly wasn't because she had asked me to mop. I could do more strenuous things than mopping. It was just her whole demeanor—the way she had spoken to me with no dignity, as if I was not human.

I mopped the living room, the hall, and the kitchen, then I went and threw out the dirty water on the patch of grass behind the kitchen. I was rinsing out the mop at the outside tap when she appeared behind me.

"*Heh!* Who asked you to throw the dirty water on the grass? Don't you know there is bleach in it? Do you know how much we pay to keep this grass like this? Bush girl! Do you think this is your dirty village where you do things any which way? Look here, if—"

"Magajia, what is it?"

I looked away from Magajia to the tall boy who had appeared behind the house. He was in a pair of white shorts, a blue polo shirt, and white sneakers. He had a tennis racket in one hand.

"Isn't it this new girl who just came here? Amerley or whatever it is she calls herself! She's been here not even ten minutes, yet she's provoking me. She messed up the kitchen, the hallway, and the living room with mud, and then she came here and poured bleach on the grass!"

While she was talking and pointing at the patch of grass, the boy looked at me and smiled. He put a finger to his head and rolled it, indicating she was crazy. I smiled. Magajia turned and caught me smiling.

"*Eh?* So now I'm a comedian, *eh*? This is all funny to you—I've become a comedian! I've become Funny Face, *eh*? Master Zaed, warn this girl, warn her or else I won't be responsible for my actions!"

She turned away from us and marched back into the kitchen.

The boy turned to me and offered his hand. "I'm Zaed. I see you've met Magajia."

I wiped my wet hands on the back of my skirt. A mistake I realized too late. I'd later have white streaks on my blue dress.

"I'm Amerley, and I'm sorry about the grass. I didn't know there was bleach in the water."

He shrugged. "It's just grass. No one even comes here anyway. So you're the new girl."

I nodded.

"Magajia was my dad's nanny. She thinks she's God around here. My dad keeps her around because they're sort of related. You know, mother's cousin's nephew's friend's grandmother's uncle's..."

I laughed. It was just like with Auntie Rosina and me.

"Don't take her seriously. Her bark is worse than her bite."

I nodded. I liked Zaed. He was funny.

Nii Okai appeared. "Master Zaed, Timothy is ready to take you."

"Tell Magajia I've given Amerley the rest of the day off. Then show her around and take her to her room," Zaed said to Nii Okai.

"Yes, sir," Nii Okai said.

"If you can't do it, get Priscilla to do it when she comes back."

"Yes, sir."

I stood there watching a sixteen-year-old instruct someone who had to be at least twenty.

"I'll see you around," Zaed said.

"Yes, sir," I said. My place in the household had become very clear to me.

Nii Okai had to take one of the dogs to the vet, so it fell to Priscilla, the other help, to show me around. She came in with another one of the drivers just when Nii Okai had been taking the dog out. Priscilla wasn't as tall as me, though she was nineteen.

She was short and stout. She had on a long weave, which she held in a ponytail on the top of her head. She was in stylish black trousers and a white blouse, which were the colors of our uniform. It was a good thing Amerley-mami had bought me a black skirt and a white blouse.

"*Ei*, so you've come?" she said when she got out of the car. She didn't wait for me to reply before adding, "Help me get these things out, will you?" She instantly reminded me of Sheba. I could tell she was one of those people who say whatever is on their mind.

She had been to the market, but the types of food she brought back told me it wasn't the type of market where traders displayed their wares on the ground and there were piles of garbage on the pavement. Magajia wasn't in the kitchen when Priscilla and I unpacked the things. There were four different types of cereal, Ovaltine, packs of fruit juices, sardines, sausages, different types of cheese, condensed milk, corned beef, spaghetti, rice, pancake mix . . . it was almost like Priscilla had walked into a shopping mall and picked some of everything. The vegetables and meats were a whole thing unto themselves. I didn't know half of their names.

Priscilla laughed when she saw the look on my face. "That was how I looked the first time I came here too. Can you believe this is only for one month?"

My eyes opened wider, though I didn't want to appear to be "bush."

She just laughed and began putting things away. "Have you met anyone yet?"

"Nii Okai, Magajia, and Master Zaed."

"*Ei*, you've met 'the enemy of progress' already? What did she do to you?"

I narrated what had happened with the mop water.

"That's how she is to everyone, don't mind her. But Nii Okai is nice. He's Madam's driver. As for the others, I don't really like them. They don't talk to me and I don't talk to them."

"I thought Nii Okai was the only driver."

"No. There's Timothy, he's Miss Zarrah and Master Zaed's driver. Mr. Iddrissu's driver is Abdul. General has been driving himself since he turned eighteen and got his driver's license."

"Who's General?"

"Mr. Iddrissu's adopted son. His real name is Omar, but his father was a general in the army. He died when General was small and Mr. Iddrissu married his mother, but they divorced. The mother also got sick and died. By that time Mr. Iddrissu had already met and married Madam. General didn't have any relatives, so Mr. Iddrissu adopted him. You can't miss him. He walks around without a shirt on to show off the lion tattoo on his chest."

"I didn't know Auntie Rosina had a stepchild."

"It's only in name. He doesn't listen to anything she says. He's the reason most of the house helps don't stay. I think he just thinks up things to torment them and make them quit, and I hear he's hit some of them before."

"How long have you been here?"

She scrunched up her face in concentration. "Sixteen months next week."

"Why have *you* stayed?"

"The pay is good and there really isn't much work here. Some of the other places I've worked—my sister, don't go there. So how much are they paying you?"

I shrugged. "I don't know. The money has already been paid to my mother."

"*Ei*, so don't you get anything? It's you who will be working."

I thought of the ten-cedi note Amerley-mami had thrust into my hand.

"No, nothing."

"Hmm. This one, *dɛ*, true monkey de work, baboon de chop. Why should you be doing all the hard work while someone else enjoys the fruits of your labor?"

"Auntie Rosina has promised to enroll me in a fashion design school when I finish."

Priscilla snorted and continued putting the things away.

"Besides, I don't mind working so my sisters can get a better life. It's only for two years."

"As for me, what I earn is mine. The agency takes ten percent but I keep the rest."

"What about your family?"

"What about them?"

"Don't they get anything?"

"I beg, am I the one who asked my parents to have children they couldn't look after? In my family, it's everyone for himself, God for us all. My younger sister has a sugar daddy; one of my brothers is an apprentice *fitter*; and as for the two older boys, they went to Tarkwa to do *galamsey* two years ago, no one has heard from them since. Everyone warned them against going to mine illegally, but they just followed some boys from my village and now no one knows where they are."

I liked Priscilla even though I didn't know her well, but I couldn't get over how she didn't care what happened to her siblings. A sister who was younger than her already had a sugar daddy? And she was standing here saying it the way someone might say their younger sister was in junior high school, like it was normal. I couldn't understand that.

"So is Madam really your aunt? Do she and your mother have the same parents?"

"No. My mother's grandmother and her mother's grandmother were in-laws or something like that. I'm not very sure of the connection."

"I beg, if you know what is good for you, don't go about calling her Auntie Rosina in front of guests or even in front of her children, especially Miss Zarrah."

"What are they like—the family?"

"Oh, Master Zaed is okay. He even talks to me from time to time. Miss Zarrah is like this, like that," she said, flipping her hand back and forth. "Sometimes she's very nice, other times you won't believe she's only twelve. And when I say she's nice, I don't mean to me. She pretends I'm invisible. The first time I came to the house, she asked me what my name was. To tell you the truth, I didn't even finish class four before I dropped out of school. All my life everyone had called me Princilla. So when she asked I said, 'Princilla.' She asked me to spell it. I said—P-R-I-S-C-I-L-L-A."

Priscilla paused, and even though the incident had occurred over a year ago, I knew she was still hurt.

"Do you know what that *nyatse nyatse* girl told me?"

I shook my head.

"'You must be dumber than you look. You can't even pronounce your name right.'" She shook her own head as she spoke.

"What did her mother say?"

A bitter look came into her eyes. "Her mother? What will she say? You think that woman cares that I was humiliated and made to look stupid by her daughter?"

If my sisters or I talked like that to anyone who was older than us, Amerley-mami would have given us a dirty slap.

"Look, I know you say you're related, but let me tell you the truth. Madam has no control over her children. She can't tell them what to do. If she does—trouble!"

"How about their father?"

"What father? Is he ever around? He leaves home by six in the morning and comes back after ten at night if he's in Accra, but most of the time he's not even in the country. He's away on business. He's just an ATM, giving them money, money, money. That Miss Zarrah, you should see the clothes she has, she wears them once and gives them away. You're lucky you're almost the same size. You can get some nice things."

I glanced at the blue *fos* dress I'd worn. That morning in our room at Teshie, it had appeared pretty and I'd seen the looks of envy on my sisters' faces, but standing here in the opulence of the Iddrissu household, I could see what it actually was—a faded blue secondhand dress.

"As for—" Priscilla began saying, but Magajia chose that moment to walk into the kitchen.

"Always gossiping! Always gossiping and yet you wonder why you're not progressing in life," she said as she walked past Priscilla.

"You"—she pointed at me—"Madam will see you now. She's in the living room."

"Thank you, auntie," I said.

"Hey wait! What would make you think that you and I share the same blood? Never call me that again, you hear?"

I nodded. I had only said "auntie' as a sign of respect; I hadn't meant anything familial by it. Priscilla rolled her eyes and continued unpacking the groceries.

"Are you a lizard? I open my mouth to speak to you and you nod."

"I'm sorry, Magajia, I won't call you that again."

"And you, I hope you know the palm fruits will not pound themselves," she said to Priscilla as I walked out of the room.

I found Auntie Rosina in the living room, just as Magajia said. She was lying on the sofa with her feet up and was going through the newspapers. She was in an African print dress. The dress was well above her knees. Her face was made up and her hair cascaded down the sides of her face. I knew it was Brazilian hair. I'd seen it so many times on TV. The curly, silky hair framed her face. She still smelled of jasmine and orange blossoms.

"Oh, Amerley, I'm so glad you could come." She sighed and laid the newspapers aside. "I'm sorry I couldn't meet you when you came in, but I get these terrible migraines in the mornings and the doctors say the best thing to do is to sleep them off. How are you?"

"I'm fine, auntie," I said, forgetting all about Priscilla's piece of advice.

"Ah ah, that's another thing. I know we're related but you can't call me 'auntie' in this house. The others will think I'm favoring you, so you'll call me 'madam,' okay?"

"Yes, aun—madam."

"Good. Magajia will show you what to do. It's not easy. There's so much to do and no one appreciates the effort I put into running this household. They think it just happens by magic."

She put a well-manicured hand to her chest and took in a deep breath. Her fingernails were painted baby pink. She wore three rings on one hand and a gold bracelet dangled from her wrist. She exhaled noisily and repeated the process three more times.

"Amerley, get me my pills, they're over there in that cabinet."

I went to the cabinet and opened it. Bottles of pills lined the shelves.

"Bring the one with the green cap and the other one with the pink cap."

I took the bottles to her.

"Madam, should I get you some water?"

"Yes, yes, and tell Magajia to make some light soup for me, I'm really not feeling well today. Tell her to use goat meat."

I went to the kitchen and relayed the message to Magajia. Priscilla got out a glass. She put it on a tray and added a bottle of Evian bottled water.

"Don't open it till she asks you to," she whispered.

I nodded and took the tray back to Auntie Rosina. She held two blue pills in her hand and one white one. She swallowed the pills, lay back on the sofa, and closed her eyes. Her dress rode up another two inches. If it went up any more, I'd be able to see her underwear. I stood there holding the tray and wondered if I should take it back to the kitchen.

"Pour me a glass, will you?" she said after about five minutes.

I set the tray down and poured the water into the glass and offered it to her on the tray. She took a sip of the water and gave it back to me.

"Tell Magajia to prepare some *apem* and *abom* with a little *mankani* and some boiled *koobi* for my lunch. Ask her to add some smoked herrings, salmon, two boiled eggs, and a lot of *kpakpo shitɔ*."

She lay down and her eyelids fluttered shut. "These days I have no appetite at all, hmm. Tell her not to use so much palm oil like she did last time. The doctors say I have high cholesterol."

"Yes, madam."

"You may go now, Amerley. I think I'll just lie down for a bit."

CHAPTER 9

I began working the very next day. My duties in the Iddrissu house included scrubbing the bathrooms once a week. In Teshie, scrubbing the bathhouse we shared with the nine other families had also been my duty when it was my family's turn. The bathrooms in the Iddrissu household were paradise in comparison. For one thing, there was no green mold or algae on the walls. There were no worms between the tiles on the floor, as there had been between the oyster shells on the floor of the Teshie bathhouse. People didn't pee in their baths or defecate there, as they did in Teshie when the line in front of the public toilet was too long. I could sleep on the bathroom floors of East Legon and not fear I'd pick up an incurable disease.

I started with Zarrah's room first. Priscilla had already been there to vacuum the carpet and dust the furniture. I was amazed at how large her bedroom was. It was bigger than our single room back home. Her bed was bigger than Amerley-mami's. I was told to change the bedsheets every week. Her favorite color was lavender, and everything in the room was a shade of it—from the curtains to the carpet to the walls.

I paused in front of her walk-in closet to marvel at her clothes, bags, belts, and shoes (Zarrah could have filled a department store with what she owned). Afterward, I went to the bathroom. Her bath products filled two shelves in the cabinets. Most smelled like fruits and flowers. I was still cleaning her bathroom when she came in and lay on her bed. She switched on the flat-screen TV and began watching a movie.

I greeted her, walked to the main door where I had left the bleach, and returned to the bathroom. As soon as I closed the bathroom door behind me, she got up and sprayed air freshener in the room. On my way out twenty minutes later, she said, "You smell so much, use a deodorant. Next time, come and clean when I'm not around."

Madam, who had been passing outside her door, heard what she said and entered the room. "That's not a nice thing to say."

"But it's true! She smells! Kristin and Aseye will be coming here later. Imagine how they'll feel if she comes in. It will be so embarrassing!"

Madam sighed and said, "Amerley, you can go now."

I went to Zaed's room next. I didn't linger there for fear of him coming in and also telling me that I stank. I tried not to stare at the posters of tennis stars that lined the walls of his room or at his bookshelf that was bulging with books. I just walked through the door and headed straight to the bathroom. Zaed was neater than Zarrah. I'm sure he rinsed his walls after each bath. He also had bottles of shampoo, liquid soap, and shaving cream in a cabinet.

Omar's—General's—room was painted black. On the walls were pictures of lions. There was one picture of a roaring lion. You could even see the tongue and fangs. I didn't venture anywhere near his bed. Priscilla told me she had cut herself once when she had been vacuuming. She'd not been wearing any shoes. Omar had broken a glass and had not cleaned up the pieces. She had also warned me about Omar's tendency not to flush the toilet after using it, so that no matter how hard you tried, you couldn't avoid looking into the bowl. I don't think the smell bothered him.

That night as I took my bath, I scrubbed my armpits with lemon, hoping that whatever *smell* I had would disappear. The next morning as I set the breakfast table, Zarrah whispered to Zaed, "I have to hold my breath anytime she comes around."

After that first meal experience, I begged Priscilla to take my place whenever it was mealtime. At the end of the month when Madam gave me my first pocket money, I used it to buy the same brand of deodorant Zarrah herself used. Zarrah stopped complaining.

"What am I going to do?" Priscilla said, coming into the room we shared in the servants' quarters. Nii Okai had a room to himself. The other driver, Timothy, didn't live on the property. Abdul only came around when Mr. Iddrissu was in town. He didn't live on the compound either.

"Magajia will kill me for sure when she finds out I didn't get this blouse altered for her."

Priscilla and each of the drivers were given a day off once a week. Priscilla usually spent hers at the hairdresser's getting her hair and nails done. She had left the house at 4 a.m. that morning and was just coming back home. It was a little past 10 p.m. She had micro braids that reached all the way to her waist.

I didn't have a day off, but weekends with the Iddrissus were typically not busy unless they were hosting a dinner or had friends over. I usually had the day to myself once my chores were done. The best thing about the weekends was getting to speak to Nikoi. There was a landline in the servants' quarters, but since Nii Okai and Priscilla had their own phones, I was the only one who waited for calls on it. I couldn't make any calls, but I could receive calls. Nikoi called me every Saturday night at 8 p.m. from a phone booth at a filling station not too far from our house in Teshie. Sometimes he had my sisters and Sheba with him. Tsina had a phone, so I could reach Nikoi, but I preferred waiting for him to call me on Saturdays. The one and only time I had used Priscilla's phone to call Tsina so I could speak to Nikoi, Priscilla had made me pay her for the phone credits I had used. Nikoi's calls on Saturdays were the highlight of my week. They were also the only way I kept up with what was happening in Teshie.

"I totally forgot. Where am I going to get someone to do what she wants?" she moaned as she dropped onto her bed.

"Your hair looks nice," I said, both in a bid to console her and because it was true. The braids were very neat and even. Not a stray hair in sight.

"I know, right? she said, swinging her head. The motion made the braids swish like a curtain around her. "This is the style Nana Ama McBrown had on her show last week."

"Isn't it painful?" I asked, looking at the fine partings they had made on her scalp.

"Not one bit. The woman who does it has soft hands. You hardly feel a thing. It's just that she takes forever to do them. And she works alone. I had to sit for twelve hours. That's why I went early, so we could start and finish early, and in my haste to leave I forgot Magajia's blouse."

"What does Magajia want done to her blouse?"

Priscilla took out one of the shapeless blouses Magajia favored and brought it to me. "She says the armholes are too tight. She wanted the seamstress to loosen them a bit."

I took the blouse from Priscilla and examined the sleeves. There was enough material for me to make the necessary adjustments. "If you'd like, I can do the alterations."

"Do you even know how to sew?"

"Yes. I'm quite good."

"Are you sure? Magajia will have a fit if she finds out I forgot to take the blouse to her seamstress, but she'll skin me alive if she finds out you did it."

"She won't know if you don't tell her. I can do this. It's quite simple actually. I'll be done in no time. If I finish and you don't like it, you can send the blouse to the seamstress tomorrow and tell Magajia the seamstress couldn't finish it because their lights went off."

Priscilla didn't look convinced but she allowed me to proceed. While she took a shower, I unpicked the stitches around the armhole and held the fabric together with pins. I threaded a needle and was done with one sleeve by the time Priscilla got out of the bathroom.

"Let me see," she said, coming to stand behind me as I worked.

I showed her what I had done.

"My goodness, you can really sew. It looks just like machine stitches. Wow. You're really gifted."

I shrugged. "I used to do alterations for people all the time when I was in Teshie."

"Did they pay you?"

"I didn't charge them. Most of them were my neighbors and I let them give me what they felt was enough."

Priscilla sucked her teeth. "Why? Don't you like money?"

She picked up her phone and started texting. "I'm going to tell all my friends about you. Anytime their madams or daughters need alterations, they'll bring them to you. We'll run a business. You'll do the alterations and I'll get us customers. We'll keep ten percent of our earnings to buy new needles and thread and whatever else you'll need, then we'll give ten percent of what we charge to the other house helps who bring us their madams' things, and we'll split the eighty percent fifty-fifty. Agreed?"

"But will we make enough?"

"Of course we'll make enough. Magajia gave me fifty cedis for this thing that you've done." Priscilla took her purse and gave me twenty-five cedis. "As for rich people, they don't value money. You wait and see the money we'll be making."

"But won't the madams be angry when they find out the jobs are coming to me?"

"They won't know. They are all like our madam. 'Priscilla, send this to my seamstress, let her take in the waist by an inch. It isn't tight enough,'" Priscilla said, imitating Auntie Rosina perfectly. "When I bring it back and it's the way she likes, do you think she's going to call the seamstress and ask her if I really did bring the things to her?"

"I'm not sure about this."

"Don't worry about anything. I'll handle it. Just imagine, you might even be able to buy your own sewing machine from the money you make."

It was the thought of owning my own sewing machine that made me agree to her plan. "I'll do it on one condition."

Priscilla frowned. "What condition?"

"We'll give ten percent to the house helps who bring us the clothes, but we'll save all of the ninety percent and use it to buy the sewing machine and other items I will need. Only after that will we start sharing the eighty percent fifty-fifty."

Priscilla's frown deepened. "That's not fair, at the end of the day you get to keep the machine and I get nothing."

"Yes, I will get to keep the machine, but we'll be able to double or triple the clothes we do if we have a sewing machine. I could have been done with the alterations on this blouse in five minutes instead of the one hour I spent using a thread and needle. And just think, we could offer a same-day service and charge double."

Priscilla bit her bottom lip as she thought about what I had just said.

"Okay, that makes sense," she said, offering me her hand to shake. There was a glint in her eye when she said, "But since I brought this first customer, I keep my ten percent."

She took five cedis off the twenty-five cedis she had kept for herself and gave me the twenty-cedi note. And just like that I began saving for my own sewing machine.

CHAPTER 10

I finished scrubbing Zaed's bathroom and toilet and lingered to read the titles of books on his shelf. Amorkor would have drooled if she had been here. I had never met a boy who loved to read as much as Zaed did. The truth was, apart from Amorkor, I hadn't met anyone else who loved to read just for the sake of reading.

I noticed *The Blinkards* on his shelf and pulled it out. The copy was brand new—it was nothing like the tattered copy they had given us in school. I opened it to one of my favorite pages and was reading when Zaed walked in.

I was so surprised I dropped the book. I thought he'd gone to his tennis lessons. What would Madam do to me if she heard I had been snooping in his room? Magajia would give me a good scolding, that was for sure.

"I didn't touch anything, I was just looking at the book."

Zaed looked from me to the carpeted floor where the book lay.

"The copy we were given in school was very old and some pages were missing. I was checking to see what parts I'd missed."

I picked up the book and tucked it back into its place on the shelf. "I'm sorry, sir. It won't happen again, I promise." *Please don't report me to Magajia.*

Zaed walked past me and took the book off the shelf. "Here, you can have it. Just return it when you finish."

I stood there just looking at him. Not only was he not going to report me, but he was also actually giving me the book to read.

"Thank you, thank you, sir."

He smiled as if he were very tired. "If we're going to be friends, you can drop the 'sir, sir' thing. Just call me Zaed."

I shook my head. "I can't. Magajia will kill me, but thank you for the book."

I turned and was about to leave when he called me back.

"Sit, talk to me."

"I have work . . ."

He picked up the intercom and told Magajia he had work for me to do. He told her to assign my duties to either Priscilla or Nii Okai.

"Sit," he said, waving to one of the chairs. He lay on the bed. "Talk to me about anything. Just keep talking, don't stop."

"What about, sir?"

"Anything. Tell me about your family."

My family? I didn't know where to start. I told him about how sometimes I wished I had been a boy so that Ataa could have stayed home and I could have continued my education.

"Do you believe in karma?" Zaed asked.

I shook my head. "I believe God has a plan and a purpose for everyone."

He sat up on his bed and looked at me. "Please don't tell me you're one of those born-again people. I don't need that right now, someone preaching at me."

"I am."

He laughed but there was no humor in it.

"So you read your Bible and go to church and believe that 'all things work together for good'?"

I nodded. I had lived in the Iddrissu household long enough to know that no one there took religion seriously, apart from Magajia, who spread out her prayer mat in her room and prayed five times a day. Mr. Iddrissu was a lapsed Muslim. Auntie Rosina was a lapsed Christian who never made it to church on Sunday mornings because of her migraines. None of the three children went either.

"You know what the white men who brought Christianity to Africa use their church buildings for now? Discos and clubs. And we have taken their religion and swallowed it hook, line, and sinker."

I shrugged. That made him angry. He went to his shelf and pulled out two books. One was on evolution, and the other was on the big bang theory.

"Science proves that this is how we came into this world! What proof do you have? If he's there, prove it!"

I didn't know why he was angry with me. What had I done?

"I can't see the wind either, but that doesn't mean it isn't there."

He covered his face with his hands. "My goodness, I can't believe how naïve you are! The wind? That's your proof?"

"It's not just the wind, it's everything. The stars in the sky, a smile on a child's face, flowers and trees and animals. The sea, the beach—everything around me proves to me that there is a God. These things didn't just happen."

"What good does believing in God do you? Does he hear your prayers? Is this what he wants for you, his 'children'? To be poor? To be a maid? To serve other people?"

"I might not like my present condition, but that doesn't mean God doesn't care or that he doesn't hear me when I pray."

"If there is a God, where is he when bad things happen to innocent people?" he said, and I could see tears in his eyes. "My best friend got shot yesterday. I didn't even know. I showed up at the tennis court and he wasn't there. I called the house and someone told me armed robbers broke into their house and shot him, just like that. He died before they could get him to a hospital. If there's a God, where was he when that happened? Why didn't he save him? Jeremy never hurt anyone. He was a good guy. He never did anything bad. He was like you, born-again. Where was God? Why didn't he save him?"

"I'm sorry he died, but if he was saved, then he's with God right now. He's in heaven."

"And if there's no heaven?"

"Then he didn't miss out on anything."

He turned away from me and banged his fists on the wall so hard they began to bleed. He started to cry. I didn't know what to do. I slipped out of the room. It was almost 11 a.m. I put my ear to Madam's door. Migraines or not, her son needed her. I hoped cutting her sleep time short by one hour wouldn't cost me my job.

There was no sound coming from inside Madam's room. I knocked twice. Nothing. I turned the knob and entered her room. The cold air hit me like a force. The curtains were drawn, but fingers of sunlight stole between gaps in the curtains and lit up portions of the room. I tiptoed to her bed. She lay on her back, a black sleep mask over her eyes. A bottle of Evian water was on her side table. She was snoring softly.

I called her name but she didn't budge. I reached over to her shoulder and gently shook her.

She snapped off the mask. Her eyes struggled to focus on me in the dark room before recognition broke through her sleep-filled mind.

"Madam, it's Master Zaed, he's crying. His best friend died."

She was out of her bed and out the door in a flash. I sighed in relief. I had done the right thing by waking her.

As I went back downstairs, I peeked into Zaed's room. He sat crouched in a corner of the room, his head buried between his legs. His body was racked with sobs. Madam was kneeling by his side. She had her arms around him. She was whispering something into his ear and rubbing his back. Whatever she was whispering only made him cry harder. I slipped away before either of them noticed me.

That night when Nikoi called, I told him what had happened and how I'd been scared Madam would scold me for waking her up, but how later that evening she had come to thank me instead.

"Her child was hurting, of course she'd want to know about it," Nikoi said.

"It just struck me how different she and Amerley-mami are, that's all."

"Don't go making comparisons, Amerley. You have enough to eat, a roof over your head, and clothes on your back. Your sisters have the same. Be content with what you have."

I twirled the cord around my finger and sank to the floor beside the phone side table. "I'm not being ungrateful, I just . . . Sometimes it's hard not to be bitter, you know?"

"I know," Nikoi said. "But if you think about the unfairness of life—what did your madam's kids do to deserve an easy life, what did we do to deserve ours—if you keep thinking about things like that, you'll just be sad and bitter all the time. It's hard to believe, but we're better off than some people."

I knew what he said was true, but living with the Iddrissus had opened my eyes to so many things. It just didn't seem fair.

"How are my sisters?"

"They are fine. Amarkai boarded my *trotro* on her way to school on Wednesday. She said Amorkor will get a prize at the end of the term in English literature."

My heart warmed. "That's not surprising. All she does is read. How is everyone else?"

Nikoi chuckled and I could hear the laughter in his voice as he said, "I think Ofoe-mami misses you. She keeps complaining that your sisters don't buy her *kenkey* anymore. She asked when you'd be back."

I laughed. "The girls are scared of her. She's too harsh."

"Speaking of harsh people, how is your Magajia?"

"She's the same. Always finding work for you to do if she finds you idle."

"How's the business going?"

"Not bad. I fixed two buttons on a shirt for one of Priscilla's friends' masters today. The shirts were not even torn. One button had come off and the other was hanging by a thread. The man was going to pay one hundred cedis to a tailor to fix the buttons for him."

"*Ei*. One hundred cedis?"

"Uh-huh."

"So no one in their house had a thread and needle?"

"Nii, I don't know for them."

"I'm happy for you. At this rate, you will get your machine in no time, and then you can help me buy my taxi."

I laughed. "It's not really my doing. It's Priscilla. She's a very shrewd businesswoman. I don't even know how she knows so many people. Some of her friends have started bringing me their own clothes as well."

"Drat," Nii whispered.

"What is it?"

"I have one minute remaining on this calling card."

"Say hello to my sisters for me when you see them, and please congratulate Amorkor for me."

"I will. I'll call you next Saturday."

"I'll be waiting. Have a good week."

"Have a good week too."

"I—"

Beep-beep, beep-beep, beep-beep, the dial tone sounded in my ear.

"I love you," I said into the disconnected earpiece at the same time that I saw the door handle to our living room turn.

Priscilla and Nii Okai had both gone out and I had locked myself in. The door handle turned again.

"Who's there?" I called out as I went to the window. We had an intercom, and if anyone in the main house needed us, that was what they used.

I pulled the curtain back and looked out just in time to see the retreating figure of Omar. What did he want? Why was he leaving? Why did he not knock? He and his siblings had never set foot in the servants' quarters since I had been there. Maybe he had been coming to see Nii Okai and just realized it was his day off. That was the only explanation that made sense. I double-checked the locks on the door and went to bed.

CHAPTER 11

The Iddrissus threw a surprise birthday party for Zarrah when she turned thirteen. It was Madam who threw the party; Mr. Iddrissu was out of town. That morning, Timothy took Zarrah and Zaed to the dentist. Zaed needed a filling and Zarrah had an appointment with her orthodontist. When Priscilla told me Zarrah's braces cost almost eight thousand cedis, I thought she was joking until she showed me the receipt, which she'd found in the garbage can. Eight thousand cedis just to have your teeth straightened! I still couldn't believe it.

By the time they came home, Zarrah's friends from school had arrived. The decorators and caterers had turned the lawn into something straight out of TV. I had never seen anything like it in real life. The DJ had already set up. We could hear Zarrah's screams from inside the car before she even got out.

Madam went to hug her. A few aunts and uncles also fussed around her. Her friends soon surrounded her, and she was shrieking in delight as she saw who had shown up.

"You! You! I can't believe you didn't say a word! I was so surprised!" she said, punching Zaed's arm playfully.

"Ouch," he said, rubbing his arm. "Mom said I wasn't to say anything. Besides, isn't that the point of a surprise birthday party?"

She screamed when the video guy came to stand in front of her. "I've got to change!" She ran into the house and her friends and relatives laughed. She came down twenty minutes later, all glammed up in a short sheath lavender dress and nude heels. She even had makeup on her face. Madam had hired a makeup artist for the occasion. This time when the video guy stood in front of her, she smiled and posed for him.

I stood near the doors and directed people to the bathrooms. It was my job to make sure the toilets were clean, that there was enough toilet paper and soap, and to mop the floor after a guest came out. I missed out on most of what happened outdoors, but from time to time I snuck over to the windows to look through. The music was so loud it made the windows rattle. Everyone seemed to be having a good time. Madam was in her element, throwing her head back and laughing and demurely accepting compliments on how she looked "not a day above thirty." You'd have thought it was *her* birthday. The birthday girl herself came indoors to change three times into different lavender-colored outfits before the day ended.

Almost everyone who came brought her presents. It was Priscilla's job to receive them and give the guests a souvenir in exchange for the gift. Zarrah's friends received a bottle of designer perfume. The adults each got a bottle of champagne.

Later, after Zarrah had made a wish and blown out the candles on her cake, I saw Zaed come in through the front door. I took up my position in front of the guests' bathroom. He noticed me and said, "You should get something to eat. Aren't you hungry?"

"I'm fine, sir," I said.

"Go on . . . go and get a snack or something, I'll show people the way."

I smiled and shook my head. My job didn't only entail showing people the way. Somehow I couldn't picture him with a toilet brush scrubbing the toilet. Anyway, Magajia would have my neck if she saw me anywhere other than where she had designated.

"I ate before the party started," I lied.

"You sure?"

"Yes, sir."

"Should I get you anything? A Coke maybe?"

I shook my head. Even drinking water on the job was a cardinal sin in Magajia's eyes. Anyway, who would want to eat or drink while standing outside a bathroom?

"I'm fine, sir, thank you."

"Well, okay, see you later then." He walked past me and hopped up the stairs.

A few minutes later Magajia came to me with a well-dressed young woman who was carrying a crying baby.

"Take her for a walk outside; the music here is too loud," Magajia said.

"Are you sure that's why she's crying?" the woman asked. She looked really worried and was reluctant to hand over the baby. "Shh, Aseda, it's okay," she cooed to the baby.

"She's just sleepy, and all this noise isn't helping," Magajia said, taking the baby away from the woman and handing her to me.

"Miss Fanny, go and eat some food, relax and enjoy the party. Aseda will be fine," Magajia said as she led the anxious young woman back to the party. Even though the woman allowed herself to be led away, she kept turning to look at me and her daughter.

The baby's face was scrunched up as she kept screaming. She was dressed in a pink dress with yellow sunflowers, matching pink shoes, and had pink baubles in her hair. I jiggled her as I walked toward the gate. I had gone only two houses away before the baby stopped fussing and fell asleep. The minute I turned and started heading back to the house, the baby began whimpering. I had no choice but to keep walking to the end of the street, where there was an uncompleted house. I wished I had taken a cover cloth so I could have strapped the baby onto my back.

When we got to the uncompleted building, which was only five houses away and still within sight of the Iddrissus', I sat down on a stump under a mango tree a little distance from the road. A gentle breeze kept the weather cool, and the leaves of the tree shaded us from the sun. The street was empty. Though I had lived with the Iddrissus for almost six months now, it never failed to surprise me how different their neighborhood was from Teshie. There were no children running up and down the streets pushing old truck tires, no groups of women going to or from the market, no hawkers, no stray animals, nothing.

Even this mango tree I sat under was an anomaly. There were ripe mangoes on the branches, and so many of the fruits had fallen to the ground and begun to rot. I smiled to myself. This could never happen in Teshie. Mango fruits mysteriously disappeared from the trees when the first streak of yellow appeared. I shook my head and looked down at the baby, who was fast asleep. Her mouth was open and she kept making suckling noises. I wondered if she was dreaming of her bottle. I admired her curly black hair and the pretty dress she wore. She was one of the lucky ones. One of the ones who would never go to bed hungry, wear *fos* clothes, be sent home for school fees, or worry whether her parents could afford the rent for their house. I rocked her as she began to whimper and wondered about Sheba and her baby boy. The last time Nikoi called me, he'd told me Sheba had given birth.

I was still under the tree when the baby's mother came looking for us. Did she think I was going to run away with her baby? The other house helps who brought me clothes to be altered always had horror stories about some of the people they worked for. One girl said a tracker had been put on her phone so her madam always knew where she was, even when she accompanied the children to school. Another one said she was made to sanitize her hands before touching any of her madam's children. Another, who worked for a minister of state, said there was an armed security guard with her anytime she was around the children.

The baby's mother was far younger than Madam. She looked like she was in her late twenties. Even though she had makeup on her face, I could see the circles under her eyes. She was in a pretty yellow fitted lace dress and blue high-heeled shoes.

"She's finally asleep, huh?" she said as she approached, and sat beside me on the tree stump. She didn't even wipe the stump or anything. She just sat down and kicked off her shoes. I hoped her dress didn't get stained.

I began handing the baby over to her mother but the woman shook her head. "No, you hold her. I just wanted to get away from the music. It was giving me a headache."

I wondered if she also had pills in bottles like Madam.

"My name is Fanny Mills. I don't think I've seen you at Rosina's before."

"My name is Amerley, and I'm new."

"Naa Amerley, that's the first girl, right?"

I nodded.

"It's a pretty name." She yawned and stretched. Her rings glinted in the sunlight. Both her engagement and wedding rings were silver. I'd thought they were made only in gold.

"I think I'll just rest my eyes a bit." She leaned against the tree trunk, and in seconds she was asleep. No one had ever told me my name was pretty. It shouldn't have meant much but it did. I was surprised at how good that simple compliment made me feel. I took the opportunity to stare at Auntie Fanny as she slept. She was beautiful, but her beauty was unlike Madam's, which made you want to stop and stare. Hers was a simple, plain beauty, or maybe I was just biased because she had said something nice to me. Though there were bags under her eyes, there were no wrinkles on her face. Her skin was smooth but she had a scar above her left eyebrow.

The sun began to set and still mother and daughter slept. Guests were leaving the Iddrissu compound in their big four-by-four cars. I didn't know what to do. Would she be upset like Madam if I disturbed her nap? Would waking her up cost me my job? Even though I had initially been reluctant to work for Auntie Rosina, I loved it here. I had more than I'd ever had to eat, I slept in a comfortable bed, I was given good clothes, my mother and sisters were doing well, and I almost had enough money to buy my sewing machine. It was a good life and I didn't want to throw it away.

I thought about taking the baby to Magajia, but what if Auntie Fanny woke up and discovered we were gone? Would that upset her? Besides, I couldn't just leave her sleeping by the side of the road like this, could I? I was still thinking about what to do when an extremely good-looking man walked out of the Iddrissus' house. He scanned the street, spotted us, and started walking toward us. The man was fine. He was tall but not overly built. His head was bald but he had a thick beard. He was in a blue-black caftan and trousers and a pair of leather slippers. He smiled when he was close enough to see that both Auntie Fanny and Aseda were asleep. When he smiled, dimples appeared in his cheeks.

"My sleeping beauties," he whispered. He took his phone out of his pocket. "Is it okay to take a picture?" he asked.

I nodded. He took several pictures of his "sleeping beauties" and put his phone away.

"I'm Joojo Mills. Thank you for looking after them. I'll just get the car and tell Rosina we're leaving."

I nodded again. Joojo Mills was a dream. A few minutes later he drove down to where we were in a black four-by-four car. Auntie Fanny woke up when the car came to a stop.

"It's time to go," Mr. Mills said, helping her to her feet.

"I was just resting my eyes," Auntie Fanny said.

"You were fast asleep," Mr. Mills said with a chuckle, and his dimples made an appearance.

"I'd just closed my eyes," Auntie Fanny insisted with a smile.

"I have evidence to prove otherwise," Mr. Mills said, taking out his phone.

Auntie Fanny laughed so hard she slapped her thigh when she saw the pictures, but then she clamped a hand over her mouth and turned to make sure she hadn't woken up Aseda. Mr. Mills just stood there grinning. Auntie Fanny took Aseda from me and strapped her into her car seat and climbed into the back with her. Her handbag and Aseda's diaper bag were also in the back. Mr. Mills climbed into the car and opened the passenger door for me. "Come on, we'll drop you."

"No, it's okay. I'll just walk."

"We'll feel better knowing you got home safe," Auntie Fanny said from the backseat.

I climbed in beside Mr. Mills, and in no time at all we were at the Iddrissus' house.

"Thank you so much for your help," Auntie Fanny said.

"Yes, thank you for looking after my girls," Mr. Mills added.

I got out of the car and waved goodbye as they drove away. I wanted what the Millses had. Not their money and possessions—though that would be a bonus—but the relationship between Auntie Fanny and her husband. It was so clear that Mr. Mills treated his wife as an equal. I desperately wanted that for Nikoi and me.

CHAPTER 12

Later that night, after everyone had left, Zarrah opened her presents. Priscilla and I stood to the side to collect the discarded wrapping paper. Zarrah had received a kente cloth from Auntie Rosina and Mr. Iddrissu. We all knew it was Auntie Rosina who had chosen it. Mr. Iddrissu had probably forgotten it was her birthday. The cloth was woven with lavender and gold threads. I was sure it was custom made for her. Kente cloths in lavender were not common. The cloth came with a lavender handbag and wedge shoes made with pieces of African print cloth. Both of them bore the label *House of Style*, the fashion design school I hoped to be enrolled in.

Zaed had given her the *Twilight Saga* book set. "Seriously, Zaed? Books?" she said, and rolled her eyes.

"I thought you loved the stories," Zaed protested.

"Duh, I loved watching the DVDs but I don't want to read the stories. I have enough reading from school."

"My bad," Zaed said, popping the bubble wrap that had been around the handbag.

General hadn't been home the entire day, but he'd left her a card.

She tore it open. A ten-cedi note fell to the ground. "Seriously, what am I supposed to do with this?" she asked, picking the note up from the ground. "Why? Does he want me to buy two sticks of kebab or what?"

"Give him a chance, he's trying," Zaed said.

"Trying would be if he had bothered showing up for the party," Auntie Rosina said, snatching the card out of Zarrah's hand and throwing it into the growing pile of garbage. "I reminded him about the party this morning, but what does he do? He gets her a cheap card and puts ten cedis in it. For what? I've had it with that boy! Amerley, get me my pills!"

By now I knew which pills to get depending on Auntie Rosina's mood. By the time I came back with the tray with the bottle of Evian water, a glass, and the pills in the green and brown bottles, Zarrah and Zaed had gone to their rooms. Zarrah was probably on her phone with a friend, and Zaed was probably playing a video game or reading a tennis magazine or one of the new books he'd bought. There was a pile of items at the foot of the sofa—T-shirts, a necklace made with local beads, plastic bangles, a pair of sandals, and all four of the *Twilight* books. Priscilla was gathering the torn wrapping paper, the ribbons, and the card from General.

"Thank you," Auntie Rosina said, taking the tray from me,

"and get rid of those things there," she said, pointing to the pile of items. "She doesn't want them."

"You mean I should throw them away?"

She shrugged. "Take what you want and throw the rest away."

When I went out with the things, Priscilla was waiting for me.

"I want the necklace and the sandals."

I handed them over to her, thinking of how Amorkor would love the books, how good Amarkai would look in the T-shirts, and how Tsotsoo would be delighted with the plastic bangles.

"Come, let's go and have our own party before Magajia comes to look for work for us," Priscilla said, leading the way to the servants' quarters.

The servants' quarters were far enough from the main house for us to play the music loud without disturbing anyone. Even before we opened the door we could hear D'banj singing "*I like Nadia Buari cuz he no de eat* gari . . ."

"Ah ah! Me, I've started without you! Why did you keep long like that?" Nii Okai asked when we entered the room.

"*Ei*, money is sweet!" Priscilla said, taking a samosa off the tray and stuffing the whole thing into her mouth.

The leftover food was on the center table in the living room.

Nii Okai had heaped his plate full of food. There was a bit of everything on it—*jollof* rice, meatballs, coleslaw, *waakye*, a ball of *banku*, grilled tilapia, samosas, and two chicken drumsticks. A generous amount of *shitɔ* capped the pyramid on his plate. By his side were a bowl, a bottle of Guinness, a can of Coke, and a bottle of Alvaro. He had poured all three drinks into the bowl and he drank deeply from it.

"Rich people are enjoying life," he said, sucking the marrow out of a chicken bone.

Priscilla lowered the volume on the CD player and tuned in to TV3, where a soap opera was showing. She took a ball of *banku*, two grilled tilapia fish, and some *shitɔ* and settled in to watch the TV.

"Is that all you'll eat?" Nii Okai asked, staring at her plate in surprise.

"Take your time. This one is only going to prepare the way. This *oyibo* food, if you don't take care, it will deceive you. You'll think you've eaten *ah-mah*, but then in the night you'll get *nketenkete* and will have to wake up to eat something."

My plate was a miniature version of Nii Okai's without the *banku* and in reasonable portions. I sat cross-legged on the floor beside Priscilla, who was chewing the tilapia bones. On the soap, the heroine of the show came out of a club. The guy she had been flirting with but whose advances she had rebuffed followed her and kept to the shadows.

"*Woaa hwɛ!* As for girls, you look for your own trouble. See this *yɛyɛ* girl. Where is she going in the night dressed like that?"

"Shut up your dirty mouth!" Priscilla said, only it came out sounding like "Sharrap your dery maf" because she had her mouth full of food.

On the TV screen, the man grabbed the woman from behind. He stuck a knife at her throat and threatened to kill her if she shouted. He laid her on the ground and raped her.

Priscilla swallowed her *banku* and turned to Nii Okai. "Are you saying it's her fault she got raped?"

"Eleven p.m. at night—any decent girl would be in bed. What is she doing out of her house? And dressed like that too! She only got what was coming to her!"

"Idiot," Priscilla said. "She said 'no' when the man asked her if she wanted to sleep with him."

"*Ho!* But everyone knows that when girls say 'no' they actually mean 'yes,' and look, she's just lying there. She's not even screaming or fighting back. It's not rape if you don't scream or fight back."

When Nii Okai finished talking, he put the bowl to his lips, took a large gulp, and burped loudly.

"She's just lying there because she's in shock. When you're in shock, you freeze. Don't you know anything?"

"*Eh koraa*, it's not real rape. She knows the man and was flirting with him. Real rape is when a stranger does it."

"So you think she's lying there enjoying the fact that the man is violating her simply because she knows him? Amerley, please talk some sense into this fool for me!" Priscilla said, drawing me into their argument.

I didn't know what to say. In Teshie when someone got raped, most people shared Nii Okai's views. They would say she should not have been out late or worn whatever it was she had worn. They said only "loose" girls got raped.

"Mr. Mills's wife, Auntie Fanny, came to talk to us at the agency. She said we were to report to them if anyone touched us without our permission or harassed us and they'd take the person to court for us, free of charge," Priscilla said.

"As for those women lawyers, they're taking this 'human rights' thing too far, but we all know nothing will come out of those cases. The families always settle out of court," Nii Okai said.

"But that doesn't mean they shouldn't report."

"God considers people, *paa*," Nii Okai said, talking with his mouth full. "If I were him, women who wear shorts, leggings, tight pants—no heaven. Women who paint their faces and nails—no heaven. Women who wear bikinis, G-strings, and see-through clothes—no heaven. Short skirts and dresses—no heaven. Sleeveless clothes and any clothes that show breasts—no heaven. Women who insist their husbands wear condoms during sex— no heaven. Condoms are abortion."

Priscilla watched him with her mouth wide open. Then she shook her head.

"If you believe all of that, you are dumber than you look."

I smiled to myself when I realized where her line had come from. It was the same thing Zarrah had told Priscilla when she asked Priscilla to spell her name.

Nii Okai went on eating as if Priscilla hadn't said anything. On TV the woman had gone to a hospital. The doctors had informed the police about the rape.

"How about the men?" I asked.

"What about them?"

"What would they have to do for God to deny them heaven?"

"Ah ah! Isn't it women who cause men to sin? Right from Eve till now, women have been tempting men!"

"What she means is, what about men who walk around bare-chested and show off their six-packs and things? Aren't they tempting women?" Priscilla asked.

Nii Okai snorted. "The Bible says the man is the head."

"What does that have to do with anything?" Priscilla asked.

But Nii Okai hadn't finished talking. "*Woaa*, look, now she's going to talk to the police! Who will want her when people get to know about it? Who will want her now that she's been spoiled?"

Nii Okai's views surprised me. Even though he was a city boy, and supposedly enlightened, his thoughts mirrored those of people, like my father, who blamed all their woes on women. The girls in my neighborhood who had been raped quietly disappeared to other places. People used to point at them and warn

131

children about what staying out late and drinking and smoking would lead to. On the one hand I believed it wasn't their fault they had been raped, but on the other hand I blamed them for putting themselves in situations that had led to their rape. But saying God should punish women for wearing pants and insisting on the use of condoms was too much. I avoided the discussion and continued eating my food. I pitied the woman who would make the mistake of falling in love with Nii Okai. No wonder he was still single.

Priscilla couldn't take it anymore. "Nii Okai, if you can't talk sense, SHUT UP!"

The landline rang and I jumped up to answer it. I had missed Nikoi's call at 8 p.m. It was now 9 p.m.

"Hi! Nikoi?"

"Where were you?" he shouted. "You know I always call at eight on Saturdays."

"It was Zarrah's birthday. Auntie Rosina threw a big party for her. We just finished cleaning up."

He was silent.

"Nii?"

"So were there a lot of people?"

"About a hundred. Kids and their parents. You should have seen the food. They—"

"So all those rich kids came with their drivers, huh?"

"Yes. Some parents dropped off the kids themselves. Some had their drivers bring them and—"

"And what were you doing?"

"I was in charge of keeping the toilet clean, and then I had to babysit someone's child. Why all these questions?"

He was silent for a while, then he sighed. "I just keep thinking you'll meet someone else. Someone better than me."

"*Oww*, Nii, that's not going to happen. Everyone was tidying up. I couldn't get to the phone at eight."

He sighed again. "There are a lot of people waiting to use the phone booth. I'll call you next week." He didn't even wait for me to say "bye" before hanging up.

I replaced the phone in its cradle and took my plate of food to the kitchen. I didn't want to hang out with Priscilla and Nii Okai anymore. I had lost my appetite. I went straight to my room. Nikoi's phone calls were the highlight of my week. I missed him so much. I missed talking to him and cuddling up with him on the beach. How could I get him to understand he had nothing to fear?

CHAPTER 13

"You went to bed before you could tell me about Mr. Mills last night," Priscilla said. Priscilla and I were cleaning the kitchen. We had cleaned the entire house. Magajia said all the people who had walked in and out of it the day before had left their germs behind. I was on my knees scrubbing the floor. Priscilla was mopping up behind me.

I yawned. I hadn't slept well. I was worried about Nikoi. Something was off with him. Last night when he called it was as if he wanted to pick a fight with me. I didn't know what to do.

"So?" Priscilla prodded. "What did he say when he met you?"

I told her what had happened when Mr. Mills came to check on his family last night.

Priscilla had a huge crush on Mr. Mills. I might have had one too, but mine was just a little, teeny-tiny crush. He was gorgeous, but more than that he was such a nice person. He and his wife both were.

"He's so, so cute. I wonder if he has a brother."

I raised an eyebrow.

"What? A girl can dream."

I snorted and went back to my work.

"As for their baby, she is too spoiled. They never put her down. When she does kɛ and opens her mouth to cry, her parents jump like the world is going to end. They pamper her too much. Someone is always carrying her."

"She'll grow out of it. They should have begun leaving her to lie down on her own when she was younger. Now she's used to people carrying her."

"I feel sorry for Auntie Fanny. She's clueless when it comes to that baby. You should have seen her when she first had Aseda. She was even afraid to put her down to sleep by herself. Her parents are in the UK and Mr. Mills's mother wasn't in favor of their marriage. When Aseda was born, she didn't even go and visit them until the baby was two months old. And when she did visit, she refused to hold the baby."

I didn't know how anyone could look at Aseda and not instantly fall in love with her. "How do you know this? Were you there?"

"Their house help, Jennifer, is my friend. She told me. We're both registered with the same agency."

It was a pity that neither Auntie Fanny's mother nor her mother-in-law were there to help her with the baby. In Teshie, when a woman had a baby, she and the baby went to live with her mother. If her mother was dead, then they went to live with her mother-in-law or an older aunt or female relative.

"No wonder Auntie Fanny was so tired. She slept under the mango tree when she came to look for me."

"But she's a lucky woman. Her husband adores her."

I nodded. That was true. He had seemed like a nice man. We were still working when General walked into the kitchen. He didn't even spare us a glance. I don't know where he had gone or how he'd managed to get mud stuck to the soles of his sneakers. He walked straight to the fridge, opened it and took out two cans of Coke and a plate of cold pizza, and went up to his room.

Priscilla was fuming. I kept my mouth shut tight. The kitchen floor was tiled; it would be easy to mop. It was the fact that he had tracked mud right through the living room, up the stairs, and to his carpeted room that infuriated us.

"Dear Lord, you have to prepare a special place in hell for people like that boy," she said, looking up at the ceiling as if she could see God.

"Let's just get this done before Magajia comes back. You know how she gets."

"Guess what?" Priscilla said, barging into our room two months later. The smile on her face was from ear to ear. The only thing that made Priscilla this excited was money. We almost had enough saved to buy an electric sewing machine. I was teaching myself to sew by watching videos on her phone. Of course, Priscilla being who she was, she charged me for each video I watched. She didn't agree to my suggestion that we treat it as a business expense. I paused the video I'd been watching and looked at her.

"*Ehhh*, have the Iddrissus offered you a raise?"

"I wish."

"We've got a big order?"

"Nope. Something even better."

What could be better than money for Priscilla?

"I give up."

"The Millses are coming for dinner on Friday!"

I shook my head. "You do realize he is already married, don't you?"

"Yes, I know, but—"

"A girl can dream," we said together.

It wasn't just the Millses who showed up on Friday night. There must have been fifty other people at the cocktail reception the Iddrissus hosted in honor of one of Mr. Iddrissu's South African partners. Magajia had made sure every surface in the house had been scrubbed or polished to perfection. Priscilla and I had been on our feet all day. A live band had arrived earlier and set up by the pool. Madam had hired a catering firm and they came with their own waiters. Magajia was in charge of helping the caterers set up and get whatever they needed from the house. Priscilla was on bathroom duty, and once again I was in charge of Aseda.

"I'm so glad to see you, Naa Amerley," Auntie Fanny said, transferring Aseda to me. Auntie Fanny was in a short black dress. She had on red high-heeled shoes and bright red lipstick. Aseda was in a blue and white romper. "The night of Zarrah's birthday, she slept through the night. We didn't hear a squeak out of her."

I positioned Aseda on my hip. She was chewing on a bunch of plastic keys.

"I hope the music doesn't disturb her," Mr. Mills said, coming into the guest room with Aseda's diaper bag. He was in a black caftan and black loafers. "How are you, Amerley?"

"Fine, thank you." They both remembered my name. It was such an insignificant thing, them calling me by my name, but it meant a lot to me.

"I'll come back to feed her in about an hour. We got here before we realized *someone* had forgotten to take her milk out of the fridge," Auntie Fanny said, looking at Mr. Mills.

"Good thing Mummy's equipment is always ready, right?" Mr. Mills said, putting his arms around his wife and planting a kiss on her lips right in front of me.

"My lipstick," Auntie Fanny protested, but she leaned into her husband and they continued kissing.

I averted my gaze. Had they forgotten I was there? I cleared my throat. They broke apart like two children who had been caught doing something naughty and stared at me with sheepish smiles.

"We'd better join the others," Mr. Mills said, taking Auntie Fanny's hand. "See you later, Amerley."

I put Aseda on the bed when her parents left, but she scrunched up her face and started crying. I shook my head. Her parents had spoiled her too much. She was one of those babies who want to be held all the time. She didn't know how to be on her own. I picked her up and sat down. She started crying again. She only stopped when I got up and started walking around the room.

"Hey, I can't be walking up and down with you for two hours! We'll have to sit at some point."

She gurgled and blew a spit bubble in my face.

"Nope. You can't bribe me with air kisses."

Aseda pouted. She dropped the plastic keys, grabbed onto the bone ring on Nikoi's mother's chain that I still wore around my neck, and put the ring in her mouth. A stream of spittle trickled down the side of her mouth. I balanced her on my hip and opened her diaper bag. It was packed with three changes of clothes, toys, rattles, and two books. You would have thought they were staying for the entire weekend instead of just two hours. I found a packet of wipes and cleaned her mouth.

I had practically raised Tsotsoo by myself, so I knew a lot about babies. But Aseda had decided I could not lay her down on the bed or even sit with her in my lap. After another failed attempt to sit down with her, I lifted her up so we were eye to eye and said, "You're too little to be this wicked." She smiled and stuffed a fist into her mouth. I couldn't even be angry at her, she was so cute.

Auntie Fanny knocked on the door in an hour's time as promised. Aseda started whimpering and struggling to free herself from my arms, holding out her hands to her mother. She must have known it was time for her feeding because she didn't even fuss once when Auntie Fanny sat in the same armchair I had tried sitting in. She kicked and flung her arms while Auntie Fanny unzipped her dress.

"Patience is a virtue," Auntie Fanny said, smiling at her daughter. Aseda latched onto the breast and sucked like she had been starved for a week. I used the time to slip away to my room to get a cover cloth. Auntie Fanny was burping her when I came back. The minute she left, I strapped Aseda onto my back. Her hands and legs were both covered by the cloth. She wriggled in protest and began fussing, but I jiggled her up and down and in minutes she was fast asleep.

I unstrapped her from my back and with great care laid her down to sleep on the bed. She scrunched up her face when her back touched the bed, but I rubbed her tummy and cooed at her and she settled back to sleep. I lay beside her, grateful to be off my feet, and arranged pillows on her other side so that she didn't roll off. I closed my eyes, intending only to "rest" them, as Auntie Fanny had the night of Zarrah's party. I don't know when I dozed off.

I woke up to the smell of cigarette smoke. I knew right away that someone was in the room with us. I stiffened and tried to pretend I was still asleep, but my heart was beating so hard I could barely breathe. Sounds from the reception drifted into the room, so I knew people were still outside. Aseda's steady breathing assured me she was still asleep. I wondered if one of the guests had come into the room. What did they want? Didn't they know cigarette smoke was bad for babies?

I forced my eyes open. General was sitting in the chair Auntie Fanny had sat in when she had breast-fed Aseda. His eyes were expressionless as he stared at me. The hairs on my arms and the back of my neck stood up. He continued staring even when I sat up and straightened my clothes. I didn't know what he wanted. Would he report me to Madam for sleeping?

He blew a puff of smoke in my direction. I coughed and waved it away. "The smoke is not good for the baby."

His expression didn't change. He continued sitting there, smoking, flicking cigarette ash on the carpet and staring at me.

When the cigarette was down to its nub, he ground it on the wooden arm of the chair, stood up, and walked out.

I leapt up and locked the door behind him. Then I opened the windows. I didn't like General. No one did. Well, maybe Zaed, but Zaed liked everyone. The rest of his family just tolerated him, Auntie Rosina barely. She often took her pills when he was around. She and Mr. Iddrissu argued constantly about him but nothing changed. General came and went as he pleased and did what he wanted. No one could discipline him. There was something about him that made me uncomfortable. Thankfully, he stayed out of my way.

I got a washcloth from the bathroom and cleaned the ash from the carpet. I had just finished washing my hands when there was a knock on the door.

"Amerley?" Auntie Fanny called out, and there was a hint of worry in her voice.

"Just a minute," I said, hurrying to unlock the door.

She had a frown on her face. "Why was the door locked?"

She entered the room and checked on Aseda.

"I didn't want people walking in and disturbing her. Someone came wanting to use the bathroom." I had no idea where the lie had come from or why I was protecting General.

Mr. Mills, who had come in behind Auntie Fanny, sniffed the air. "Is that cigarette smoke?"

I opened my mouth, prepared to tell another lie, but Auntie

Fanny lifted Aseda and cradled her. "It must have come from outside. Those South Africans smoke like there's no tomorrow."

"Think she'll sleep through the night again?" Mr. Mills asked, running a finger over Aseda's chubby cheeks.

"I hope so. Amerley seems to have a way with her."

"I wish she'd take to Jennifer the way she's taken to Amerley," Mr. Mills said.

They thanked me and left the room. I straightened the bed and was taking the soiled washcloth to the laundry room when Madam sent Priscilla to get me.

"What did you do?" Priscilla asked. "Mr. Mills and Auntie Fanny were standing with her. I heard them mention your name but I couldn't hear what they said."

My heart thrummed. Was I in trouble because I had locked the door? Or was it because I had left their baby in a room filled with cigarette smoke? I left the washcloth on one of the washing machines and went outside, where indeed the Millses were standing next to the Iddrissus. Most of the guests had left, though a few were still standing around with drinks in their hands, talking and exchanging business cards.

"Madam?" I said, standing with my hands behind my back.

Dear Lord, please don't let them send me back. I like it here. I really like it here. I promise not to complain about how unfair life is. Please let them not sack me. Please.

Madam was in high spirits. I'm sure the reception had been a raving success. She'd be the talk of her peers for the next few weeks, and that made her happy. She was in a shimmering gold gown that clung to her curves in all the right places. The only pieces of jewelry she wore were a pair of dangling teardrop diamond earrings and her engagement and wedding rings. Mr. Iddrissu stood next to her looking immaculate in a black suit.

"The Millses have something to ask you," Madam said.

I turned to Auntie Fanny and Mr. Mills. They didn't look angry. Mr. Mills was actually smiling.

"Would it be okay if you watched Aseda, maybe once or twice a week?"

That was it? That was all they wanted? They just wanted me to babysit Aseda?

"Jennifer's no good with her. Anytime we leave them together, we come back to find Aseda has been crying the entire time we were away. Fanny is going back to work. It's part time for now, but we've been worried about leaving Aseda with Jennifer."

I was so relieved, I was speechless.

"We'll pay you for your time, of course," Auntie Fanny said.

"Of course," Mr. Mills said like it was a no-brainer. The thing was, I would have agreed to babysit Aseda even if they did not pay me.

I looked at my madam and her husband.

"It's your decision," Madam said.

"Okay," I agreed.

"Super! We'll send Raul to pick you up. It will just be two times a week for now. From nine a.m. to noon. I don't think I can bear to be parted from her longer than that," Auntie Fanny said, kissing the still-sleeping Aseda's rosebud lips. Mr. Mills put his arm around Auntie Fanny, and they beamed at me like I had just turned water to wine.

CHAPTER 14

I began waking up earlier on Mondays and Tuesdays so that I could get all my chores done before Raul, the Millses' driver, came to pick me up. Their house was not as large or flamboyant as the Iddrissus', but anything larger than a single room impressed me. The house was painted the same cream and brown colors as the Iddrissus'. Instead of flowering plants, they had a big vegetable garden in their backyard where tomato, lettuce, cabbage, okra, onions, mint, and cocoyams grew. There were a few plantain, orange, lemon, and avocado trees at the borders of the vegetable garden, and just next to the kitchen window the vines of a passion fruit plant climbed up a trellis.

Their living room was like a shrine to Aseda. Pictures of her were everywhere. I was surprised to see I was in one of the pictures—it was the one taken on the day of Zarrah's birthday when both Auntie Fanny and Aseda had been asleep beneath the mango tree. It was a beautiful picture. Though I was in it as a blurry person holding Aseda, I was honored they hadn't thought anything of including the help in a picture on their walls. Jennifer was also in two of the pictures with Aseda. A plaque on one of the walls read:

Speak the truth, even when your voice shakes. —Anonymous

I wanted to ask Auntie Fanny what the quote meant, but I was too shy. Though she was nice and approachable, I was still aware of the gap in our social levels. I wouldn't want her to think I thought of her as an equal and could converse with her about normal, everyday things like quotes on her wall, so I concentrated on what I was there to do—look after Aseda.

The Millses were right. Aseda just did not like Jennifer. She could be snoring in my arms, but the minute Jennifer picked her up to put her in her cot, she woke up and began screaming.

"I must have been her wicked madam in a past life or something," Jennifer once told me as she shelled boiled groundnuts and popped them into her mouth. She was taller than me and wore a nose ring. When she was done with her chores, she spent her time on the couch in the living room watching Nigerian movies. She had a room in the main house. The Millses' servants' quarters served as a storage unit. No one lived there.

Jennifer was not bothered that the Millses had brought me in to help out. "It's their money and I'm still getting paid in full, so why should I care?" she said when I brought it up.

Aseda's room was the prettiest room in the house. It was twice the size of our room in Teshie and was done in shades of pink and cream. Flowers and butterflies were painted on the walls. A wind chime hung by a window and twinkled when the wind blew. Her crib had a sheer pink canopy around it. A plaque bearing her name in cursive print was on one wall. She had a dresser of clothes, baby booties, shoes, and hair accessories that had been organized by color. Four picture albums were already full with photos of her, and she was just five months old. Stuffed animals filled two cane baskets. One wall of her room had a shelf full of baby books. A bamboo rocking chair with a couple of Ankara throw pillows was propped up by one of the windows, which overlooked the garden. Auntie Fanny usually sat there to nurse her.

Taking care of Aseda was a breeze. In her home, she often allowed me to put her down for minutes at a time or hold her on my lap when I joined Jennifer to watch her movies. I don't know what Jennifer did in the Millses' home; it was always a mess and no one seemed bothered by it, least of all her. Sometimes I'd come in the morning to find the sink full of breakfast dishes and Jennifer already at her post in front of the TV. Other times there'd be a pile of laundry for washing, and all she would say was that she was too tired that day. She was never too tired to eat, though, she was always snacking on something—plantain chips, boiled groundnuts, popcorn.

Jennifer was a terrible cook. She couldn't even boil rice properly. Usually on Mondays and Tuesdays, Auntie Fanny bought food when she came home from work. She always bought some for me. Though she invited me to eat with her and Jennifer, I always refused. I took my food back to the Iddrissus' and sometimes shared it with Priscilla and Nii Okai. Sitting down and eating with Auntie Fanny seemed too weird.

"Are you avoiding me?" Nikoi asked when I picked up the phone the next Saturday.

I sighed. It was going to be one of those nights. He was in a bad mood and I was in no mood to coddle him. It was past 9 p.m. At ten minutes to eight o'clock I'd been called to the main house to clean up Zarrah's bathroom. She was in a body-care phase and was trying out new bath products. She had filled her bathtub with water, then poured in about half a bottle of some new product that had made bubbles and overflowed the tub. I had spent thirty minutes mopping her floor.

"I was called to the main house to clean up a bath spill, that's why I couldn't be here at eight."

Nikoi was silent. I couldn't tell if he believed me or not, and frankly, at this point, I didn't care. I was tired and all I wanted to do was to go to bed.

"Are you sure?"

"Nii, I've told you why I wasn't here at eight. Whether you believe me or not is your problem."

He sighed. "I'm sorry. This is harder than I expected."

My heart melted. "I know. We have just a little over a year to go and then I'll be done. And guess what?"

"What?"

"Remember that babysitting job I told you about?"

"Uh-huh."

"It pays so well that I have enough to buy a sewing machine!"

"Really? That's great news! Well done!"

I could hear the smile in his voice, and that made me happy.

"Are you still coming home next week?"

"Yup. I'll be there in the flesh, live and colored," I said with a huge smile on my face.

The Iddrissus had given me two weeks off to go and visit my family. Secondary schools were on holiday and Madam and her kids would be out of the country for the next month.

"I still can't believe it."

"Me neither. I can't wait to get back. I miss you so much."

"I miss you too."

We chatted until Nikoi ran out of credits. I climbed into bed and dreamt of him and of my family.

After eight months, I was finally going home.

CHAPTER 15

"Sister Amerley! Sister Amerley!" Tsotsoo cried, running toward the car. She was followed by five of her playmates. I was pleased to see she was fully clothed. She even wore clean *charley-wotes* on her feet. In a corner of the yard, a group of boys who had been playing stopped to watch the car drive up to our door.

"*Ei*, see how you've become a small madam. I'm sure your sisters will do all the work in the house. You can sleep and wake up at twelve if you want to," Nii Okai joked when more of our neighbors came out of their homes to watch me get out of the car.

Amorkor got up from the veranda where she had been cooking *banku* on a coal pot. When the wind blew, it sent embers dancing around the black pot. She hugged me so tight I almost stopped breathing. The wooden paddle was still in her hand, and some of the hot maize and cassava dough mixture dripped down my arm.

"Go and finish cooking the *banku* or else lumps will form in it," I said.

"Ah, Sister Amerley, do you want to eat *banku*? Let's go and buy fried rice for you," Amorkor said.

"No, I want it. I've missed eating *banku* with pepper."

"It will be ready soon," she said, sticking a finger into the cooking dough to check its consistency.

"*Ei*, so you don't use the cooking shed at the back anymore?" I asked as I noticed the new shelves on the wall that housed most of our cooking utensils. Two sacks of charcoal had been placed in the corner of the veranda.

"No, not anymore. Nuumo has even converted it into another goat pen."

"Good for you guys, then, cooking in the rainy season was always a bother."

Nii Okai took out my bags from the trunk, and the children scrambled to pick them up and carry them to our room. He walked back to the car.

"Won't you stay and eat?" I asked.

"Magajia wants me to pick something up from Spintex for her. Maybe in two weeks when I come to pick you up."

"I hope the next two weeks don't come quickly," I said as he climbed into the car.

"It'll come, you watch and see. When you want time to stand still, that's when it flies, and when you want it to pass quickly, that's when it slows down," Nii Okai said, and drove away.

I went around the entire compound greeting all our neighbors and giving them fake smiles because I knew most of them had expected me to come bearing gifts.

"*Ei*, Amerley, is that you?" Ofoe-mami asked on her way to her stall. She was walking behind two men who were pushing a truck loaded with basins of her *kenkey*, cane baskets of fried fish and shrimps, and paint buckets of red and black *shitɔ*. "*Ei*, see how you've become a fine girl like that."

I smiled blandly at her and mumbled something about God's grace. One of the neighborhood girls came to pour dirty water into the gutter in front of where Ofoe-mami was standing. Some of it splashed onto her leg.

"*Heh! Olu? Kwɛmɔ buului anii ni ofee*," she shouted, turning toward the girl.

I used the opportunity to slip away and returned to our room. Knowing Ofoe-mami, she wasn't going to stop until the whole neighborhood had heard what had happened.

"Where's Amerley-mami?" I asked as I pulled out a stool and sat by Amorkor on the veranda. She sat on a short stool in front of the coal pot. Pieces of charcoal burned bright red in the pot. Blue and red tongues of fire licked the bottom of the black cauldron. Amorkor's feet were positioned on the metal rods that supported the pan on the coal pot. As the mixture thickened, her whole upper body and arms moved in a rhythm of its own to get the *banku* smooth and soft. I was proud of her. I had taught her well.

"She's still at the market. Now she leaves by five a.m. and comes back at seven p.m. Sometimes eight. By the time she comes back, she's so tired she just eats and sleeps," Amorkor said, molding the *banku* in a calabash.

"So her business is going well, *eh*?" I was glad to see the netting on the screen door had been replaced. A new welcome mat with all the letters lay in front of the door.

"Very well. Now she goes to buy the goods from Togo. They're cheaper there."

"So who's home when Tsotsoo finishes school?"

"Tsotsoo has French classes three times a week. On the other two days she has computer classes. When I finish school, I pick her up and we come home together."

"*Ei.*"

"Yes, Amerley-mami says one of her customers told her all the big-shot children know French and computer."

"How about Amarkai? What does she do after school? Why isn't she back yet?"

"Sister Amerley, do you even have to ask? She spends all her time at the clinic."

Tsotsoo emerged from the room with a glass of cold water.

"*Ei*, do we now have a fridge?" I said, accepting the water from her. I noticed it was a new glass. There were no chips or cracks in it. I drank all the water.

"Yes, a tabletop fridge. Amerley-mami makes stew and soup for the week on Saturdays," Amorkor said.

"Sister Amerley, look," Tsotsoo said, smiling at me.

"What?" I asked.

She smiled even wider. It was then that I noticed her teeth. The two front ones had grown in. They were big. About twice the size of the ones she had lost.

I chuckled. "The lizard didn't get them after all, huh?"

She shook her head.

"Tsotsoo, bring a glass plate for Sister Amerley."

"No, it's okay. Let's all eat together. Like we used to."

"Are you sure?"

"Yes," I said.

She molded a big ball of *banku* and upturned it into a bowl. She dished out two smaller balls into two different bowls—one for Amerley-mami and the other for Amarkai. Then she put the *banku* pan in a corner of the veranda and poured some water into it. Tsotsoo cleared a wooden table and put a cup and a bottle of water on it. She brought me a bowl of water to wash my hands. Amorkor heated some *bɔbi tadi* on the stove. The smell of the *bɔbi* made my mouth water. I hadn't eaten *bɔbi* since I moved to East Legon. Amorkor got out the *asanka* and quickly ground some *kpakpo shitɔ*, one tomato, and half of a small onion. I had sent Tsotsoo to buy a tin of sardines. We opened it and poured the contents into the *asanka*. The sardine oil floated on top of the pepper.

"That reminds me, Sister Sheba brought us some avocados," Amorkor said, disappearing inside. She returned with two and sliced them onto the pepper.

As soon as Amorkor put the stew on the table, I took a ball of the *banku*, molded it, dipped it into the *bɔbi tadi*, and picked up some *bɔbi*. *Banku* with anchovy stew was one of my favorite meals, but no one ate anchovies in the Iddrissu household. The ball of *banku* burned the roof of my mouth and my throat as it went down. I could feel the hot ball when it finally settled in my stomach. I used my fingers to fan my mouth and drank some more water from the glass, which Tsotsoo had refilled. I took it easy after that and blew on the *banku* before swallowing it.

Amarkai came home while we were still eating. After nearly toppling the table as she leaned over it to hug me, she washed her hands and joined us. After supper my sisters followed me into the room. I was surprised to find it had been painted and Amerley-mami had bought a standing fan. I opened my suitcase and took out the *Twilight Saga* books and some others Zaed had given me, as well as a pair of sandals Zarrah had thrown out, and gave them to Amorkor. I gave Amarkai a pair of shoes and an old book on dogs Mr. Iddrissu had thrown out. Both of them got to share a ton of Zarrah's clothes. Tsotsoo got Zarrah's old dolls, toys, and plastic jewelry. She shrieked in delight and started jumping up and down.

I put three of Auntie Rosina's dresses, two handbags, a purse, and a pair of low-heeled slippers on the bed for Amerley-mami. While my sisters rejoiced over their gifts, I took out my towel and sponge. Amarkai fetched water out of a drum on the veranda and carried it to the bathroom for me. Amorkor had already spread out her mattress and begun reading the first book in the *Twilight Saga*. Tsotsoo was on Amerley-mami's bed talking to her new toys.

I nearly fled the bathroom when I set foot in it. I'd forgotten about the green mold on the walls, the smell of urine, and the earthworms that crawled between the oyster shells. Some things had changed, but other things remained the same. I would need gallons of bleach to properly clean it.

"Don't you guys clean the bathroom? It's so filthy," I said as soon as I got back to our room.

"*Ei*, it's not even a year yet and you've gone high and mighty on us," Amerley-mami said. "Be careful or people will say you've become too-known." She had come home and was eating her *banku* and *bɔbi tadi*.

"Good evening. I didn't see you."

Amerley-mami hadn't seen or spoken to me in eight months. I had thought she'd be more welcoming. I was wrong. I wondered if she still hadn't forgiven me for the fight we'd had before I left.

"So how are you?" she asked, shaping the last ball of *banku* in her hand.

"I'm fine."

She nodded and went outside to wash her hands. Then she came back inside, took her towel, and went to bathe. While she was bathing, the lights went off.

"Ah ah, I thought they rationed light only during the day," I said. The Iddrissus had a backup generator. The lights never stayed off for longer than thirty seconds in their house.

"Sister Amerley, *paa*, this one is normal lights-off," Amorkor said, switching on a rechargeable lamp that she placed by her pillow, and continued reading.

When Amerley-mami came back, she went straight to bed. I didn't know why she was being so cold toward me. She didn't even pretend to be interested in the work I did for the Iddrissus. Was I not doing what she wanted? Couldn't she see all I was sacrificing for the family? What more did she want me to do? Even though I pretended not to care, it hurt me a lot. I lay on my mattress in the heat and waited for sleep to come.

By the time I woke up the next morning, everyone was gone. It was almost 9 a.m. I was surprised I hadn't heard them as they got ready for work and school. I took a cup of water, went behind the house, and brushed my teeth. I was on my way back to the room when someone called my name from across the compound.

"*Ei*, Amerley! Amerley! So it's true."

I turned to see who it was. It was Sheba. Her son was strapped to her back.

"*Atuu*," she said, hugging me. I hugged her back. She smelled of woodsmoke and urine. There was a wet patch on the cover cloth she had used to strap her baby onto her back. She unstrapped her son and thrust him into my hands. He had white beads around his wrists and legs and was in a white undergarment and cotton underpants, which were still wet with urine. He didn't have on diapers like Aseda. His nose was runny and mucus dripped down onto his undergarment. Sheba used the hem of it to wipe his nose.

"Ah ah! Sheba, are you pregnant again?"

She giggled. "Can you tell? I thought I wasn't showing yet."

"But he isn't even nine months yet."

She giggled some more. "It just happened. Virgin Mary, how about you and Nikoi? He won't wait for you forever. You be there, someone will snatch him from you."

"Sheba, I don't even have a proper job. Where will Nikoi and I live?"

"Oh, if you're waiting for a house and a proper job, then, my sister, you'll wait forever . . ."

Just like Aseda, Sheba's baby grabbed the bone ring around my neck with his grubby hands. It went straight into his mouth. He drooled saliva and snot onto my neck.

"Aww, he likes you," Sheba cooed, and used the ends of her cloth to wipe the saliva off my neck.

"What's his name?" I asked.

"Guess," she said, giggling.

"Nii . . ."

She shook her head before I even finished. "It's a Bible name."

"Peter?"

She shook her head.

"Paul?"

Another shake of her head. "It's an unusual name."

"Bartholomew?"

She rolled her eyes.

"Jericho?"

"Ah ah! Why would I name my child Jericho?"

"I give up. What?"

She smiled so wide I could see the spot where she had had one of her molar teeth taken out. "Hosanna."

I looked at her. "What does it mean?"

"Why are you asking me, aren't you the *Osofo Maame*? It means 'deliver us.'"

I looked at Hosanna, who was busy sucking on the bone ring, and hoped he wouldn't end up like me—having to work somewhere to make ends meet for his family.

"You should have been here for the naming ceremony, it was *spectacular*! We blocked the street from here to there"—she turned to show me—"we had a live band. I sewed *kaba* and *slit*, the fashionable style with the lace sleeves, and wrapped my head with a *gele*. You should have seen me, I looked muuaah"—she put all five of her fingers to her lips and kissed them.

"But how did you pay for all that?"

She shrugged. "Tsina borrowed money for it. I said I wanted a big naming ceremony or else the baby wouldn't carry his name. After all the suffering I went through at the maternity clinic, that was the least he could do."

I stood there gaping in disbelief. They couldn't even afford two meals a day, yet she had a big naming ceremony for her baby.

"What? *Yɛbɛwu enti yɛrenna?* Amerley, you should have been there! We had so much fun. That day when I danced, people put money on my forehead. By the end of the day I had one hundred and twenty-five cedis."

I smiled. Knowing Sheba, she'd kept all that money for herself. I doubt Tsina even got a pesewa.

"How's work?"

"It's okay apart from those *aaba ei* people, but if you give them one cedi they won't worry you again."

"I brought you some clothes."

Her eyes lit up as she followed me into our room.

Hosanna chose that same moment to pee on me.

"I told you he likes you! When a baby pees on you, it means blessings, *sɔɔ*!"

My next visitor that day was Nikoi, and I was glad I had showered and changed clothes by the time he got there. I threw my arms around him and clung to him.

"I thought you were at work!"

"I told my master I ate some roadside food that didn't agree with me. I told him I'd been 'running' since dawn."

"What if he finds out? I'm sure people have seen you here. People talk, you know?"

"Let them talk," he said, and carried me to Amerley-mami's bed. When he put me down, he slipped his hand under my blouse. I swatted it away.

"I had to try," he said, grinning.

"It's not going to change, no matter how many times you try. What's with the beard?"

He was growing a beard and mustache but hadn't bothered shaping it. The scraggly hair just grew in all directions and was longer in some parts and shorter in others.

"You like it? I hear it makes me looks sexy," he said, stroking his beard.

"It makes you look unkempt," I said, pushing him away from me, "and it itches my face."

He lifted my necklace off my chest. "You still have this?"

"You didn't think I was going to throw it away, did you?"

"It's my promise ring." He kissed me. "I thought of you every single day."

"Me too, I thought of you day and night. I missed you so much," I said, hugging him tighter.

He smiled. "I thought you'd have forgotten me by now."

"But we speak every week when you call."

He raised his hand and tucked it under his head. The smell from his armpit hit me. Was that how I'd smelled when I first went to the Iddrissus'? I took a closer look at his black T-shirt. It stank and there were dried crusts of saliva and *kenkey* on it.

"Did you use deodorant today? When was the last time you washed that shirt?"

His arm snapped back to his side and he withdrew from me. "Why? Am I smelly?"

"I don't mean it in a wrong way," I said, snuggling close to him. "You do smell a little strong."

He moved away from me. "'A little strong' was fine for you before. I've always smelled like this."

"Nikoi, please, I'm only here thirteen more days. Please don't let us fight."

I got up and went to my suitcase. "Here, I brought you some

things," I said, taking out some of General and Zaed's old clothes and shoes. Nikoi looked at me like I had insulted him and walked to the door.

"I don't need your handouts."

I followed him out the door and down to the beach where he was headed, sidestepping the clothes people had left to dry on the sand. I had missed the ocean, hearing the waves roar and the salty smell of the air. I had missed the sounds of the gulls screeching, the cacophony of voices as fishermen and fishmongers haggled over prices, and the feel of the sand on my toes, but I didn't dwell on any of these as I ran to catch up with Nikoi.

"Nikoi, wait, please wait," I said, grabbing onto his arm.

He flung my arm away and stalked down the beach.

"Nikoi, I didn't mean to insult you. You've done a lot for my sisters and me. I wanted to show my appreciation."

He turned to look at me and he looked hurt.

"My friends were right; this is not going to work."

"Nikoi, what isn't going to work?"

"We . . . Us. You've been gone only eight months and you've already changed so much."

"Me? I haven't changed. I'm still me."

"Really? I've been with you for only ten minutes and you're already criticizing me!"

"I wasn't . . . I'm not criticizing you."

"Really? First you pretend to be surprised to see me—"

"I wasn't pretending . . ."

"Yeah? So what was the interrogation about my not being at work for?"

I looked at him in surprise.

"Then you say I look 'unkempt.' Then you say I smell, and then you bring me a rich boy's clothes because suddenly the way I dress isn't good enough for you anymore."

"Nikoi, that's not true!"

"Isn't it? If you still love me, how come you never called me, not even once!"

I had tears in my eyes. "You know I don't have a phone. The landline you call me on is only for incoming calls!"

"You want me to believe those rich people didn't give you any of their old phones when they seem to have given you everything else? My friends were right!"

"Will you stop talking about your friends? This is about us!"

"I know. That's why it's best we end it now. There's no sense in prolonging this. Once you start going to your fashion school and meeting important people, it will become even worse."

I swallowed the lump in my throat. "Nikoi, I love you. I'm sorry if I hurt you, but—"

He grasped my arms. "If you love me, quit the job and come back here. You've got your sewing machine now. I've got some money saved up. We can use it as a deposit with the madam here. I'm working on a deal with a financial institution in Accra

Central—if it goes well, I'll be driving a taxi soon and I'll get you the rest of the things you want. Don't go back. Stay here with me, Amerley."

"I can't. I have to think about my sisters. I can't break Amerley-mami's arrangement with Auntie Rosina. Besides, aren't you the one who said working there was a great opportunity for me?"

"I did, but it's changing you."

"No it's not!"

He dropped his hands. "You can't even see you've changed. What will happen next time you come back? You'll think you're too good for me and dump me. There's no sense in continuing this. Let's end it now."

"Just like that?"

He looked away. "It's for the best."

Long before I'd even met Nikoi, I'd made up my mind that I'd never beg a man to stay with me if he didn't love me. I'd never be one of those girls who stopped living because a man left her.

He turned and continued walking down the beach. My hand went around the bone ring he had given me. Never in a million years had I thought it would come to this. I stood there watching him go—watching as my heart broke in two.

CHAPTER 16

I spent most of my first week at home avoiding Nikoi. That meant I didn't go to the *trotro* station or the night market. It was terrible. I'd vowed I wouldn't cry over a man, but I couldn't help it. Cry was all I did. I wore a brave face in front of my sisters and pretended to be excited at the stories they told me. I'd never known a breakup could hurt this much. My heart felt raw, as if someone had taken a grater to it and then put salt on the wound.

"Just give him time," Sheba said to me as she bounced Hosanna on her knee. I'd become Hosanna's babysitter. Sheba left him with me in the mornings before she left to hawk her goods. Sheba's milk was not enough for her son. She brought a flask of *koko* each morning when she dropped him off, and I fed it to him when he was hungry.

"How much time do you think I should give? I have less than a week left. And if he doesn't call me when I go back to the Iddrissus', how will we talk?"

"I'll talk to him. If that doesn't work, I'll ask Tsina to talk to him. He's just intimidated by how posh you have become."

Me? Posh? That was not a word I would ever use to describe myself.

"I'm not posh," I said.

Sheba rolled her eyes. "Yes you are. Look at your clothes and how you speak. Even the way you walk has changed."

I shook my head. "I'm still the same me. Nothing has changed."

She looked at me and smiled. "That's what I like about you, Amerley. You're not too-known."

I didn't agree with her but kept quiet. Arguing took too much energy. After crying over Nikoi that night, I didn't have any energy left.

"Is there . . . Does he have another girl?"

"Who, Nikoi?" Sheba shook her head. "Of course not. What would he want with another girl when he has you?"

"Maybe—"

"Maybe nothing. Do you know no one goes to use the pay phone when it's eight p.m. on Saturdays? Everyone knows that is the time Nikoi calls you. When we see him walking toward the pay phone on Saturdays, we know it's almost eight. He's devoted to you. I wish Tsina treated me the way Nikoi treats you."

If he was so devoted to me, how come he'd broken up with me?

"You getting your sewing machine probably made it worse."

"What do you mean? He was happy when I told him I'd finally

bought the sewing machine. He'd been so supportive. How could it have made things worse?"

Sheba shrugged and bounced Hosanna some more. "Men like to feel needed. When he was the one providing for you and your sisters, he knew you needed him, knew he was important to you. Now he's not very sure why you're with him, when you probably meet drivers who are better off than him every day."

"That doesn't make sense. I love him. I choose him."

Sheba looked at me in surprise. "Are you just now realizing men *don't* make sense?"

I spent the next week trying to talk to Nikoi. He was never at the station when I went there, and in the evenings he wasn't at Tsina's shack or at our spot on the beach. On my last night I tried one more time.

I heard the strings of the guitar before I even got to the coconut trees. I was so thankful I had finally tracked him down. That had to be a sign, right? If what Sheba said was true, I needed him to know he was still important to me.

I sank onto the sand beside him. He ignored me. When he finished the song he was playing, I took his hand in mine.

"I'm sorry if I made you feel like you were not good enough for me." I forced the words out. It felt like a lump had formed in my throat, and my tears were threatening to fall. "I just wanted to do something nice for you. You've been so good to my family, so good to me. Nikoi, please just give me a second chance."

"Amerley, don't . . ."

I could see the pain in his eyes. That made me feel better, but not by much. At least I wasn't the only one suffering. We could work things out. We would work things out.

"Please, Nikoi. Just give me a second chance. Maybe we should shift our calling time to nine p.m. No one has ever called me to go to the main house at nine p.m. before. I just have a little over a year left. Next year by this time, I will be almost done. Please, Nii, give us a second chance."

He clasped my hand and a flicker of hope unfurled within me.

"I'm so scared of losing you, Amerley."

"I'm right here. You'll never lose me. I choose you, Nikoi. I'll always choose you." The tears were coming down my face faster than I could wipe them away.

Nikoi gave my hand one more squeeze and let go. In that instant I knew I had lost him.

"Go back to the Iddrissus'," he said without malice. "Enroll in the design school and open your own shop when you finish. Find someone who'll love you and who won't be a burden to you like me. You deserve a good life, Amerley, and I don't want to be the one who keeps you from getting it."

"No, Nii—"

"Shh." He put a finger to my lips and kissed my forehead.

"Going back is the right thing to do, Amerley. It was selfish of me to ask you to stay. Forget about me. You'll meet someone better." He stood up and hoisted his guitar onto his shoulder.

I didn't know it was possible for an already broken heart to break again. The pain was so much deeper than the week before.

"Nii, wait," I called after him.

He stopped and turned back. He was just a few steps away from me but it felt like we were oceans apart. I put my hands around my neck to unclasp the gold chain with the bone ring he had given me.

He put his hand on mine to stop me. "Keep it. Let it remind you of me—of the love we once shared."

When Nii Okai came for me the next day, I was glad to be leaving Teshie. Maybe distance would make me forget Nikoi.

"He's an idiot," Priscilla said when I told her Nii and I were broken up. She tried to get me to go out with her so I could meet her male friends, but I just wasn't interested.

Life with the Iddrissus continued as usual. I kept busy during the day, and by night I was so tired I fell asleep the minute my head touched the pillow. There was no time to think about Nikoi.

CHAPTER 17

"*Ei*, Amerley, look at my face, look." Priscilla turned away from the mirror to face me.

"Stand still so that I can finish what I'm doing."

She stood still while I finished hemming the dress with the needle I was holding. I snapped the thread with my teeth and spat out the bit in my mouth.

"There, you're all set now."

She twirled in front of the mirror. "Today, *deɛ*, I look hot!"

I had spent the past three days altering one of Madam's dresses to fit Priscilla, and now I stood back to look at my handiwork and took pride in what I had achieved. If I could do this with raw talent, what would I be able to do once I got formal training? I hoped the next year passed quickly so I could finally start schooling at House of Style.

"Amerley, look at this black face. Don't say you don't know me when you become a big name."

I rolled my eyes, put a hand on my heart, and with a straight face said, "I promise I won't forget you."

She sucked in her tummy while I closed the zipper at the back of her dress; I only hoped it wouldn't pop open when she was out with her friends from the agency. One of the madam's friends was throwing a party for her help. Priscilla had invited me and Nii Okai, but I had declined. Sheba and my sisters had taken over calling on Saturdays. It was through them that I heard about Nikoi and what he was up to. I knew it was pathetic, but hearing about him made me feel better now that we weren't speaking. It was through them that I found out he was now driving a taxi.

Priscilla slipped her feet into an old pair of Zarrah's blue heels. Priscilla was nineteen, Zarrah was thirteen. The shoes were for a thirteen-year-old, but Priscilla insisted, come hell or high water, those were the pair she was going to wear. She cinched her look with a large blue belt and twirled once more in front of the mirror.

"Say it," she said, addressing my reflection in the mirror.

I laughed. "You look hot!"

She smiled and picked up her purse, another of Madam's thank-you items, just as Nii Okai called from in front of the door, "I'm not paying extra for the taxi!"

She rolled her eyes but yelled, "I'm coming, I'm coming!"

She applied a bit more gloss to her lips and doused herself in half a bottle of perfume.

"It's not too late to change your mind, you know? Madam and Miss Zarrah won't be back tonight. They'll stay with her sister after the wedding reception tonight and go on to the thanks-giving service at the church with the couple tomorrow. Magajia sleeps like a baby, she won't hear anything and we'll be back way before dawn."

I shook my head.

"Priscilla!" Nii Okai yelled again.

"Nii Okai, what do you want me to do for you? What? Are you the one who got the invitation? Don't rush me, I said I'm coming!"

She waved at me and walked out the door, with Nii Okai berating her loudly as he followed closely on her heels.

I checked the time. It was only 7:30 p.m. I had thirty more minutes before Sheba and my sisters would call. I lay down on the sofa and switched on the TV. As I was flicking through the channels, my eyes fell on the *Lord of the Rings* trilogy set I had borrowed from Zaed. I picked them up and walked to the main house. I'd start a new book while I waited.

The Iddrissu household was clothed in darkness. I climbed up the stairs and knocked on Zaed's door, which was partly open. Music was playing loudly from his surround sound home theater system.

It was some American rapping faster than Sarkodie. I knocked a second time and pushed the door open.

Zaed and General sat side by side in front of the flat-screen TV playing a car racing game. General saw me first and turned down the volume on the stereo. He had a lollipop in his mouth and an amused look on his face.

"You have a visitor," he said to Zaed.

General had never taken any notice of me before. If Zarrah behaved like I didn't deserve her notice, General behaved like I was invisible. Apart from that night when he had stared at Aseda and me when we were asleep, he didn't pay any attention to me.

Zaed turned to look at me. "Oh, hi, just drop them there."

I placed the books back on the bookshelf and turned to leave.

"Don't go, sit down," General said.

Then he turned to Zaed. "Your mother would be appalled at your lack of good manners. Won't you offer her a drink?"

Zaed glanced at General. He looked confused, then he pointed to one of the seats. He got up and poured a creamy drink into a disposable plastic cup and handed it me. Both of them had cups full of the drink by their sides. I glanced at the bottle, which was by General's feet. On it was written *Baileys*. I took a sip of the drink. It tasted very creamy and nice but I could still taste the alcohol. I sipped my drink and watched them play. Zaed was making all sorts of contortions with his arms, but he was losing. General sat still, elbows supported on his knees, moving his controller this way and that.

After their first game, they asked me to heat some leftover pizza for them. I went downstairs and did just that. I took along some paper plates and napkins but they ate straight from the box. General refilled my cup, which I had emptied without realizing it, and offered me a slice. Midway through their second game, General got up and said he had to pee. He handed me his controller and went into Zaed's bathroom.

I had never played a video game before, so Zaed showed me what to do. Even when General came back, he just sat back and watched me play. Though I kept losing, I was enjoying myself too. I could now understand why they both spent so much time playing games in their rooms. It was addictive. By the end of my third game with Zaed, General had refilled my cup two more times.

I heard the grandfather clock downstairs chime and remembered the phone call I'd been expecting from Sheba and my sisters. I glanced at the clock in Zaed's room. It was 9 p.m. When had eight o'clock come and gone? I jumped to my feet and swayed.

"I . . . I . . . ha . . . ha . . . havetogo," I said, and giggled when I heard myself slurring the words.

"Go where?" General asked. "It's only nine, or will you turn into something at the stroke of midnight?"

For some reason I found that very funny and laughed loudly.

"She's drunk," I heard Zaed say. "She's probably never had this stuff before."

General snorted, "Whoever heard of someone getting drunk on Baileys?"

"Notever," I agreed. "Dontdrinkalcohol."

Zaed looped my arm around his neck and supported me with his other arm. "You're going to have a massive headache tomorrow."

I found that even funnier and laughed.

"You won't think it's funny tomorrow when you're throwing up in the toilet. Come on, I'll take you to your room."

The next thing I knew I was lying on Zaed's bed.

"What's wrong with you?" I heard General say. His voice sounded like it was coming from the opposite side of the room, though I could see his face hovering over mine. "You have a drunk girl in your room and you're sending her away?"

Hands pulled down my skirt and ripped off my blouse.

"She wears waist beads," General said. "Does anyone do that anymore?"

I felt someone on top of me, then General's face broke through the fog in my brain. I heard him grunting. I turned my head and saw Zaed standing by his side and watching us before I passed out. When I came to, General was still on top of me. I felt like my insides had been ripped open. I felt my waist beads tear. I passed out again. The next time I came to, I was in my room, on my bed, naked except for the gold chain with the bone ring around my neck and a cloak of shame.

General came back to my room about an hour later with my clothes. I pulled my cover cloth tight around me and huddled as close to the wall as I could get.

"If you tell, I'll say you lied. I'll say this wasn't our first time. I'll say you agreed to it. And no one will believe you—you're just the maid."

He flung my clothes at me and left the room.

CHAPTER 18

General started calling me "mumu" a week after it happened. It wasn't that I consciously decided not to speak again, I just shut down. Not all of me, only my voice box or voice container or whatever is in my throat where the words are produced.

Sometimes I felt the words bubbling up, on the verge of spilling over, like when you'd boil cassava for *fufu* and the steam would lift the lid off and make the water spill over. Most times that's how I felt. But just when the words were about to spill out of my mouth, the temperature dropped and my throat froze. The words froze with them and I just stood there—speechless.

That afternoon, he was lying on a sofa watching TV with his family when I walked in with a tray of fruit salad. On the TV screen, Nadia Buari was shouting at John Dumelo, telling him he was a "good-for-nothing bastard." I envied her rage. I envied the way she jumped on John Dumelo and punched him in his face, on his chest, on his stomach. I envied the words pouring out of her mouth. I wished I could have done the same. The only ones watching the movie were Auntie Rosina and Zarrah. General was playing a game on his iPhone.

"Amerley, when you're done with the dishes, come and join us. This is the second part of the movie we watched two weeks ago," Auntie Rosina said when I offered her one of the bowls of fruit salad.

I nodded.

I offered the tray to Zarrah. She looked at it with disdain.

"Where's the milk? I told you I wanted mine with condensed milk. Where is it?"

I just stood there because the words "We're out of condensed milk" wouldn't come.

"What's wrong with you? Can't you talk?"

It never ceased to surprise me how this thirteen-year-old could speak to me this way. Amorkor was fifteen. At home, she spoke to me with more respect than this girl. It was Auntie Rosina who interceded.

"Priscilla says we've run out of condensed milk. I'll pick some up tomorrow. Try the fruit, it's good."

Zarrah muttered something under her breath and turned back to the TV screen.

"You're blocking my view," she said to me.

Once I moved aside I became invisible. She had no more use for me.

I took the tray to Zaed, who shook his head even before I got to him. His head had been buried in the pages of a book since I entered the room. I didn't bother trying to sneak a glance at the title, as I would have done a week ago. I didn't bother. I didn't care.

I moved to General, who tore his gaze away from his phone screen to look at me. He was bare-chested. His tattoo of a lion seemed to move as he moved his arm. It was as if the lion were actually roaring. General winked and took a bowl of fruit. He brushed his fingers deliberately over my hand. Inwardly I was screaming. Outwardly I was still me. Speechless. Silent. *Mumu.* No expression on my face.

"Is there any ice cream?"

I stared at him.

"I asked you a question."

I dropped my gaze to my feet and noticed idly that I had a broken toenail. I needed to cut my nails.

My silence seemed to infuriate him.

"*Mumu!* Answer me when I speak to you."

When he got no reply, he rose and stood right in front of me. He tipped the tray. The pieces of fruit dropped down the front of my white blouse. The glass bowls smashed on the marble floor. Pieces of fruit and juice ran under the sofa.

"Omar! Temper!" his stepmother cautioned, but General stomped out of the room.

"Amerley, please clean up that mess," Auntie Rosina said without taking her eyes off the TV screen.

I picked up the broken pieces of glass and put them on the tray before returning with the dustpan and mop. I could feel Zaed's eyes boring holes into my back. I didn't look in his direction. He got up with his book and walked out of the room. Auntie Rosina sighed. Family time had been disrupted.

In school, when we used to write essays on the topic "The Day I Will Never Forget," it was mostly about happy days like birthdays or graduations or Christmas. Sometimes it was about doing something stupid like giving your money to a man at the *trotro* station who said he could triple it if you closed your eyes and counted to one hundred. Sheba had been foolish enough to fall for that. By the time she had counted to one hundred and opened her eyes, the money-tripling man had disappeared, and so had her market money. She had refused to go home that night; she knew what her mother would do to her. Nothing my mother or any of our neighbors said could get her to change her mind. She had stayed with us for three days before going back home, and that was only because her mother had sent her a message through Vashti: "Even if you move heaven and hell, you will still come home and find me waiting." Sheba finally decided to go home and take what was waiting for her. You couldn't throw away good money like that and not get punished for it.

There were two days in my life I will never forget. The first was the day Auntie Rosina came to our house in Teshie. The second was the day a week ago here in East Legon. It surprised me how something that didn't even last ten minutes in the real world could turn my whole life around, could make me feel like I had died and been born again into a crueler, sadder, uglier world. In the real world, it was only ten minutes. In my new world, it took forever for it to be over. I felt it was more like ten years. Maybe time stopped. Maybe it didn't. Maybe I just don't know anymore.

CHAPTER 19

"Ah ah! Don't you have work to do? What are you still doing here?" Priscilla asked, coming into the kitchen, where I had been sitting and staring into space. "Aren't you going to get ready? Raul will be here soon. If Magajia sees you sitting idle like this, she'll find more work for you. 'The bathrooms won't scrub themselves, you know.'"

I got up from the chair. Last week I would have laughed at her for imitating Magajia so perfectly. Today I didn't think I would ever laugh again.

"Amerley, what's wrong with you? You've been so *leemm* lately. Why are you so down?"

"Nothing," I said, walking past her and up the stairs that led to the first floor. I could feel Priscilla watching me as I climbed upstairs, but she didn't follow me. She had a ton of clothes to wash in the laundry room.

Today I didn't pause in front of Zarrah's walk-in closet to marvel at her possessions as I usually did. I walked straight to the bathroom. Though she had left for school an hour earlier, the bathroom windows and mirrors were still covered in steam. Even when the sun was high in the sky and the ground was so hot your feet felt like you were walking on burning coals, Zarrah bathed with water that was so hot you could use it to pluck the feathers off a chicken.

The next room was Zaed's. I didn't linger there either, not even by his table, where I could see a stack of new novels waiting to be transferred to his bookshelf. I had become numb enough that I just walked through the door and headed straight to the bathroom. Tucked underneath one of the bottles was an envelope. It had my name on it. I picked it up and opened it. It contained some money and a letter that began with the words "Dear Amerley, I'm so sorry . . ." I put the letter back into the envelope and placed it back under the bottle. I didn't even bother counting the money. Did he think writing an apology letter would be enough? Or did he think if he gave me some money it would magically make everything all right? I took out the scrubbing brush. I scrubbed mechanically, thinking about nothing and everything. When I was done, I left his room.

I walked straight to General's room, and something caught my eye. My string of waist beads dangled from the edge of his wastepaper basket. I left it where it was, entered the bathroom, and scrubbed it.

Back outside, Priscilla had taken the first batch of clothes—

the whites—out of the washing machine and was hanging them on the clothesline.

"Are you sure you're okay?" she asked.

I nodded.

"Help me with this," Priscilla said, unfurling a white and yellow bedsheet. She gripped one end, I gripped the other, and we draped it over the line. She clipped on the clothespins and came to stand in front of me.

"Did something happen over the weekend?"

I stared at her and felt the tears build behind my eyes. *If you tell, I'll say you lied. I'll say this wasn't our first time. I'll say you agreed to it. And no one will believe you—you're just the maid.* I shook my head and looked away from her.

"Did you receive some bad news from home?"

I shook my head again.

"Are you still upset about Nikoi?"

I shook my head a third time as I bent to pick up the pillowcases and hung them out to dry. Priscilla continued looking at me for a minute before she picked up Zarrah's panties and hung them beside the pillowcases.

Priscilla and I had finished hanging the first batch of clothes when Magajia stuck her head out of the kitchen.

"Amerley, Raul's here. Don't expect me to pound the *fufu* tonight. If you're not here to do it, Priscilla will do it all by herself."

Priscilla walked with me to the gate. She had a partially ripe mango in her hand. She knocked it on the wall a couple of times to get it to soften up. The mango left a green stain on the white wall each time she hit it.

"Today is going to be a bad day. Magajia has been grumbling all morning. When you leave, she'll start mumbling that there's work to be done here and yet you chose to go for a ride. As if she doesn't know it's the Millses who asked for you."

She knocked the mango some more. The green stain grew larger. She took a deep bite out of it. Watching her eat the mostly unripe fruit set my teeth on edge.

"What?" she asked, noticing the look on my face. "I have been timing this mango for three days now. If I hadn't plucked it, Nii Okai would have eaten it—"

"*Heh!* Priscilla or whatever your name is! Who do you want to empty the garbage can? Do you think it will empty itself?" Magajia called from inside.

Priscilla rolled her eyes and sucked on the mango with gusto. "I think she was an army sergeant in a past life. How can one person shout like that from morning till evening? Look, you don't have to come back early. It's only one tuber of cassava and one finger of plantain anyway. I can pound it. If it was me, I'd spend every minute looking at Mr. Mills's face."

I didn't bother telling her that by the time I got there Mr. Mills was already at work. It was just Auntie Fanny and Jennifer.

"Priscilla!" Magajia screamed.

Priscilla pulled the mango seed out of its flesh. Mango juice dripped down her arm. She twisted her hand and licked it off.

"Priscilla!"

Priscilla stuffed the entire mango seed into her mouth, waved at me, and sprinted back to the house.

CHAPTER 20

I could hear Aseda's screams from the Millses' front gate. I hurried up the front stairs. Just as I raised my hand to knock on the door, it was flung open. Mr. Mills stood in front of me in a white T-shirt and a pair of camouflage shorts. His eyes were bright red. His beard looked ungroomed. They must have had a really rough night with Aseda if he was still home at this time and wasn't even dressed for work. He looked at me with reverence—as if I had some healing power in my touch. As if I were one of those preachers on TV who only have to speak and disabled people begin walking and running on the stage.

"Please come in. We took her to the hospital yesterday. They said she had a fever because she was teething—it's crazy in there . . . I don't know what's wrong with her."

He led me to Aseda's room, where she lay in her cot screaming her head off. Auntie Fanny sat on the floor by the side of the crib. She was rocking herself. Her eyes were shut tight. Each time Aseda screamed, she grimaced and flinched. You'd have thought Aseda's screams were hot needles that were piercing her body.

Toys lay scattered all over the place—teddy bears, every stuffed animal you could think of, rattles, sing-along books, and dolls. There was a laptop on one of the tables; nursery rhymes played over and over. Beside the laptop were two books. One was titled *Your Baby and You*, and had a picture of a happy smiling mom and an equally happy smiling baby. The second book lay open to a chapter on teething. So many paragraphs had been highlighted in yellow that I thought it would have been better if the entire book had been printed on yellow paper. Multiple Post-it notes had been stuck to the pages of the books. Two feeding bottles and three different pacifiers were on one of the tables. A bottle of acetaminophen syrup lay beside the crib. Next to it was a tube of gum ointment.

Aseda's face was bright red and scrunched up to let out another scream. When she opened her mouth, I could see two pink mounds at the front part of her lower gums, and just visible were the tips of her front baby teeth. I picked her up. She kicked and screamed even louder. I checked her diaper; it wasn't wet. Her temperature was up, so I stripped off her clothes and walked to her bathroom. I ran some cold water in the bathtub and gently washed her body. Her father hovered over me in the bathroom, handing me a sponge and a towel when I needed them.

When I finished, I rubbed her dry. She was still crying but

her cries were not as high-pitched as before. I sprinkled some baby powder between her legs, in her armpits, on her back, and around her neck. I dressed her only in a diaper and strapped her onto my back.

Mr. Mills joined Auntie Fanny, who was now standing beside the door. He put his arm around her shoulder They both watched me as if I was performing a miracle. Auntie Fanny was still in her nightie. The area around her nipples was wet. She was leaking breast milk but didn't seem to notice. Her hair was standing in all directions. She had bags under her eyes, which were even redder than Mr. Mills's. She kept a hand cupped over her mouth.

Mr. Mills bent down and kissed Aseda's head as I walked past him and Auntie Fanny. I went downstairs and into the backyard. I jiggled Aseda as I strolled through the garden, and gradually her screams grew quieter and settled into whimpers. I felt her body go slack and I knew she had fallen asleep. I stopped and sat on one of the steps leading to the kitchen, but she began whimpering again, so I stood up and continued pacing. As I was walking around the garden a third time, I noticed Auntie Fanny. She'd had a shower and changed out of her nightie into a sleeveless *boubou*. She sat at the top of the steps leading to the kitchen.

"I'm so jealous of you right now. You make it look so easy."

I didn't know what to say; no one had ever been jealous of me before.

"Come, sit by me. She's asleep now."

I unstrapped Aseda and handed her to her mother. Aseda pursed her lips as if preparing to let out another scream, but she didn't. Her mother gently rocked her and she settled in her mother's arms and went back to sleep.

"I never thought I'd be bad at this," Auntie Fanny said, stroking Aseda's head.

"My little sister was like that too when she was teething." I forced the words out of my throat.

"You have a sister?"

I nodded. "Three."

"Three! I wonder how your mother managed. Tell me about them."

My throat shut down again and I just sat by Auntie Fanny, not saying anything. The words didn't even bubble up in my throat as they had before. My voice was all dried up.

"Amerley, it's okay. By now you should know you can talk to me. I know you're not allowed to speak to guests at Rosina's, but this is my house and you're my guest. Don't feel shy."

My throat was still clamped shut. Auntie Fanny waited but I still didn't talk.

"Let me put Aseda to bed. There's some juice in the fridge, get a glass."

I followed her into the kitchen and picked a glass from the counter. Their fridge was a mess. There were leftover plates of everything—stews, pizza, bread, yams, palm soup, cheese, *jollof* rice, and a head of tilapia with all the bones from the body beside it. If Magajia saw this, I'm sure she'd have a nervous breakdown. I took out a carton of fruit juice. I wasn't very sure if it was fresh or not. I sniffed it. It smelled okay. I poured less than half a glass and took a small sip. It didn't taste funny. Other people's fridges were not my business. I shut it and waited.

I wanted to tell Auntie Fanny I was ready to leave. I went to wait for her in the sitting room. Mr. Mills was asleep on the sofa. He lay curled up like a baby with his mouth partly open. I don't think an earthquake could have woken him up. Watching him sleep like that, I wondered if Ataa had ever stayed up through the night with me or any of my sisters.

When I heard Auntie Fanny on the stairs, I went back to the kitchen.

"I don't remember the last time the house was this quiet," she said as she quickly braided her hair and twisted it into a bun at the nape of her neck. She washed her hands at the sink. "I don't even remember the last time Joojo and I had a decent meal."

She opened the fridge and shut it quickly. She made a face and looked at me.

"You know, it's not always like this. I don't know how Rosina manages to keep your house so spotless. With Jennifer on leave, things have been a bit hectic."

Our house being spotless had nothing to do with Auntie Rosina. It had everything to do with Magajia ordering Priscilla and me to keep it spotless.

"I have to leave," I said, rinsing out my glass at the sink.

"No, no, sit. How can I send you away without feeding you?"

"I'm not hungry."

"Nonsense. It's almost lunchtime. You're eating before you go back."

I pulled out a chair and sat at the kitchen table as she opened the fridge and emptied out half of its contents. The vegetables had turned to green slime. I wasn't sure I wanted to eat anything out of that fridge.

She put some rice into a boiling pot of water and went out to the garden. When she came back, she caught me staring at the wall clock. She had a head of lettuce, some carrots, bell peppers, and spring onions in her hand.

"You're not leaving till you eat," she said in a voice that left no room for argument.

While the rice cooked, she washed the vegetables, then chopped and stir-fried them with chunks of sausage, pieces of chicken, and mushrooms.

"Stop glancing at the clock, will you? Don't you ever get out of the house? Don't you get days off?"

I shook my head.

"What agency are you with?"

I shook my head again. None.

Auntie Fanny took the veggies off the fire and checked the rice.

"Do you have a contract?"

She saw the look of confusion on my face.

"Do you and the Iddrissus have a contract? You know, an agreement about how much you're paid, how many hours you work, how many days you get off, that kind of thing."

"We're related," I mumbled.

She stared at me, then left me in the kitchen and disappeared upstairs so fast I thought Aseda had woken up, but I couldn't hear her crying. Auntie Fanny came back clutching a sheaf of papers.

"All this time I thought you had a contract because I helped Priscilla with hers. These are your rights as a domestic help. Read through this and I'll have a talk with Rosina . . ."

I was shaking my head before she even finished speaking.

"No, I'm a lawyer . . . it's fine . . . this is my job. You have rights as a help."

I shook my head and pushed my chair back.

"Amerley, wait . . ."

I was out of the kitchen and through the living room door. Auntie Fanny's calls woke up Mr. Mills. I ran to the gate and struggled to get it to open. It had a complicated locking mechanism. I was still frantically turning knobs when Auntie Fanny appeared by my side.

"I'm sorry. It's okay if you don't want to talk about how they're treating you, but please let Raul take you back. Please." She looked like she was on the verge of tears.

"I want to leave now."

"Yes. Fine. That's okay. Let me get Raul."

She hurried past Mr. Mills, who was at the door rubbing his eyes and trying to stifle a yawn. He looked very confused. I got in the car and waited for Raul.

In minutes she was back out the door with her purse. Raul had gone to open the gate.

Auntie Fanny came to the window and pulled out a card from her purse. "Here, take this."

I shook my head.

"Take it!" She threw the card through the open window and it fell on my lap.

Raul came back and started the car.

"If you ever want to talk about it or about anything at all, call me or come here, okay?"

I looked away from her without answering. Raul drove out of their compound.

CHAPTER 21

She was crazy. She didn't know what she was asking. How could I ask Auntie Rosina for a contract after all she was already doing for my sisters and me? What did it matter whether or not I had a day off? I didn't know anyone in East Legon, where would I go, what would I do, anyway? I knew Priscilla had a contract, her agency insisted on it. It was why she got weekends off, worked eight hours a day, and got paid holidays.

Auntie Fanny! How could she even suggest something like that! It would make me look so ungrateful. Auntie Rosina didn't maltreat me. In fact, she hardly took any notice of me, and she had given me so many things—clothes, bags, shoes, jewelry, bottles of perfumes she no longer wanted. Because of her, my sisters and my mother didn't wear rags anymore and had more than enough to eat.

When Raul showed up the next morning, I told him to tell the Millses I wasn't feeling well. I'd tell Madam I didn't want to babysit Aseda anymore. I'd lose the additional income, but at least I wouldn't be pressured to ask Madam for a contract.

I did my chores and went to report to Magajia when I was done. She was not in the kitchen. Magajia was the only one of the servants who had her own room in the main house. I knocked on her door and waited for her to grant me permission to enter. There was no reply. I turned the knob and entered. Magajia was lying on her bed drinking condensed milk straight from the can. She was watching a Nigerian movie on Cine Afrik. She was startled when she saw me.

"Wasn't the door locked?" she asked, pushing the can of milk under her bed.

So that's where Zarrah's condensed milk had disappeared to.

"What do you want?" she demanded.

"Please, I've finished my chores."

"Aren't you going to babysit Aseda today?"

"No. I've quit."

She nodded as if I'd finally come to my senses.

"The beans for the *red-red* tomorrow won't pick themselves, you know?"

I made my way back to the kitchen and poured the black-eyed beans onto a tray. I went to sit in the summer hut behind the house. Next to it were two jacaranda trees in full bloom with small purple flowers.

I'd begun sorting beans when I was three years old. At the time, I would pick each seed, examine it carefully to make sure there were no holes with weevils hiding inside, and set it aside. Amerley-mami was an expert at bean sorting. Her fingers moved quickly through the pile, and in no time at all she was done. Over the years I'd become an expert just like her. As I sat under the jacaranda trees, my fingers worked while my mind wandered.

Though I had spent almost a year in this house, Auntie Rosina had yet to introduce me to the proprietor of the fashion school, even though she had visited many times. She always looked like she had stepped out of the pages of some high-class fashion magazine. She treated me like everyone else in that house. I couldn't wait to leave the Iddrissus and begin living my own life. I'd put this thing with General behind me. I would learn from it and never go into the main house when his parents and Magajia were not there. I would learn all I could from the madam at House of Style and open my own business so that none of my sisters would ever have to go through what I had been through. I still felt degraded and dirty and useless. The pain in my heart was as raw as it had been that first night, but I made a vow to myself that I would get over this. I was bigger than this. *God has a purpose for me*, I repeated to myself as tears made their way down my cheeks.

I smelled him before I saw him. I tensed and felt the fear creep into my bones. My heart began to pound. I sat still and hoped he would not notice me. I hoped he'd just smoke his cigarette and go away. Not long after I'd smelled the cigarette smoke, I heard gravel crunching on the path to where I sat.

He sauntered my way. I ignored him and with trembling hands continued what I was doing. All my attention was now focused on the beans. The pile with bad seeds remained small. Priscilla bought the black-eyed beans from a supermarket. There were very few bad beans and no weevils or stones. I didn't really have to sort the beans at all, but Magajia would insist on seeing the bad ones, so I had no choice but to sift through them.

General came to sit opposite me and blew a mouthful of smoke into my face. I held my breath and kept sorting.

"Why have you stopped talking? You'll make people suspect something."

I ignored him.

"Look at me when I talk to you."

I kept my head down. What would he do if I didn't? Rape me again when the house was full of people? He took the tray away from me and placed it on one of the chairs. He forced me to stand up. With one hand he tipped my chin back until our eyes met. He glared at me. With the other hand he took the cigarette out of his mouth. I blinked back the tears that were threatening to fall. I would not show him I was afraid. He brought his head closer to mine and kissed me on the lips. I jerked away from his touch. He gripped my jaw firmly, lifted the cigarette, and forced the lit end through the bone ring that lay nestled between my breasts. I screamed but his hand shot up from my jaw and clamped my mouth shut. The tears flowed down my face. I started shaking. My heart started beating really fast.

"I just love a woman with hair on her chest. It's so sexy," he whispered, and kissed my ear. "I'm going to take my hand off now. If you scream, I'll hurt you more. If anyone comes by, I'll say we've done it before. I have a witness, remember? Zaed will back me."

I held back a scream.

"Do you understand?"

I nodded.

"Seriously, can't you talk anymore?"

He took his hand away and pushed his body against mine. I stood rock-still. He brought his hand to my face and ran a finger over my lips. His tattoo peeked out from under his sleeve.

"*Mumu*, you'll make some guy a good wife one day. Imagine this to be your rehearsal. The old man is leaving tomorrow. His wife and Zarrah will go to that stupid wedding on Saturday. It'll just be you and me and Zaed. He'll swear I spent the night playing video games with him," he whispered.

His parents and sister would be away, but Magajia and Priscilla would be around.

As if he could read my mind, he said, "Magajia won't hear a

thing. She sleeps like a dead person, and I heard Priscilla say she's taking the day off. Be at the side door at nine p.m. If you're not there, I'll come to you."

This was a nightmare. *Oh God, this can't be happening. I can't go through that again. I can't.*

He threw away the cigarette, held my jaw, and forced his tongue into my mouth. It tasted of ash. Zaed's words played in my head. *If there is a God, where is he when bad things happen to innocent people?*

He continued probing my mouth with his tongue and groping me. I bit down hard until I tasted blood—his blood. He screamed and pushed me away from him. A film of blood covered his teeth, and blood gushed out of the cut on his tongue like a fountain.

"You whore! You filthy whore! How dare you?"

He put his hand to his mouth and it came away bloody. The blood seemed to infuriate him further. He hit me and sent me reeling. I crashed onto the chair with the tray of beans. The tray fell and sent beans flying in all directions. He stamped his foot on my chest. The force of the stomp broke the bone ring in two. He kicked me twice in my stomach. Then he held my head and used it to hit the ground so hard I passed out.

CHAPTER 22

My entire body hurt but the pain in my lower abdomen was brutal. It was the first thing I felt when I regained consciousness. It felt like I was being stabbed with knives. I had to take shallow breaths. I tasted blood in my mouth and spat it out. I didn't know if it was my own blood or General's. I sat up gingerly. Every muscle in my body ached. I felt a sharp pain in my abdomen and doubled over. General must have gone on kicking me even after I'd fallen unconscious. I don't think I had ever felt more pain in my life, not even the night of the rape.

As I struggled into a sitting position, I slipped on some of the bean seeds. Magajia would kill me for sure. I would have to gather the beans and sort them all over again, but I hurt too much to do anything about it. She would expect them to be soaked in water overnight. What would I tell her? I struggled into a standing position and limped over to the servants' quarters. I'd worry about the beans later. Magajia couldn't do any worse than what General had already done to me.

As soon as I pushed open the front door, Priscilla shouted from our room, "Amerley? Madam just gave me one of her dresses, I need you to—"

She came out of our room to meet me and froze when she saw the state I was in.

"Oh my goodness. What happened to you?" she said, helping me over to one of the sofas.

Even lying down was painful. Tears came into my eyes as she lowered me onto the cushions.

Tears appeared in Priscilla's eyes. "Who did this to you?"

I closed my eyes and drifted off into unconsciousness once more.

When I came to again, I was still on the sofa but Priscilla wasn't the only one standing by my side—Auntie Rosina, Magajia, and Nii Okai were with her. Priscilla was using a damp towel to mop the sweat off my face.

"Who did this to you?" Magajia asked.

"Do you even have to ask?" Nii Okai muttered.

"General," I whispered.

"Oh, that boy will kill me!" Auntie Rosina said, collapsing into a chair and burying her hands in her hair. "What does he want from me? What haven't I done for him? From now onward no one will clean his room, leave it like that. I'm fed up!"

"Priscilla, help her up. I'll get the car," Nii Okai said, moving to the door.

"Car for what?" Auntie Rosina asked, getting up.

"Madam, won't we take her to the hospital?"

"Are you crazy? The doctors will want to know what happened. They'll call the police. We can't make this a police case!"

"Madam, he does this every time," Magajia said, speaking up for the first time. "He always does something to the girls to make them leave. As for this one, he's gone too far. Madam, we have to send her to the hospital."

"Magajia, are you talking back to me?"

"Madam, no, but Amerley doesn't—"

"Don't think because I let you have your way around here we're equals. Don't you ever forget your place! I only tolerate you because of your master!"

The room was deathly quiet apart from the sound of my labored breathing.

"We'll give her some painkillers and make her rest. I don't think anything is broken. She'll be better in no time at all. Priscilla, get me my pills."

Priscilla just stood there looking at Auntie Rosina.

"Are you deaf? Get me my pills and a bottle of water."

Priscilla went to do as she was told.

"Okai, heat some water for me. Magajia, get her a towel and some antiseptic."

Both of them left the room.

Auntie Rosina sat by me on the sofa. "Amerley, did he . . . did he rape you? There's no one here but us, you can talk to me. You can tell me."

I nodded my head but had to stop because the movement made me dizzy.

"Yes. Zaed was there too. He saw everything."

She covered her mouth with her hand. "What? When?"

"Last week."

Tears sprang into her eyes. "Zaed? Are you sure Zaed was part of it too?"

Again I managed a slight nod of my head.

Auntie Rosina shook her head. "No, you must be mistaken. Zaed would not stand by and let something like that happen. You're confused, Amerley."

"Just ask him," I whispered.

I saw the look on Auntie Rosina's face and knew her mind was made up.

"Amerley, you are confused. General raped you but Zaed wasn't there."

There was no point in arguing. I didn't have the energy to argue.

Auntie Rosina stroked my head. "You can't tell anyone, okay? This will ruin us if it gets out. Mr. Iddrissu's business will be hurt. Please, keep it to yourself. When you get better, I'll enroll you in the fashion school."

Priscilla came back with all of Auntie Rosina's pills. Auntie

Rosina selected five different types of pill and forced me to swallow them. The taste of blood in my mouth made me gag.

"Okai, carry her to her bed. Magajia, make some chicken soup for her."

Priscilla screamed when Nii Okai picked me up. "There's blood on the cushions!"

I must have passed out again after that. When I woke up again, I was in my own bed. Magajia was wiping me with a towel. She had tears in her eyes. I could see the bruises—they were dark red with a purple tinge. They were all over my abdomen. I saw Priscilla flinch every time Magajia touched my body. She left the room sobbing. I passed out once more.

CHAPTER 23

The pain in my side was the first thing I felt when I woke up. I couldn't breathe deeply because it hurt too much. My head felt like it was about to split open. The room I shared with Priscilla was quiet, but I could hear raised voices coming from the living room.

"How can you even say that?" Amerley-mami said. She was sobbing. "She's still urinating blood! She needs to be in a hospital. She's been like this for a whole week! We have to take her away from here!"

"Are you blaming me for this? Am I the one who sent the girl here? Did you ask my permission?" Ataa retorted.

"Ask your permission? Where have you been for over a year and a half? What sort of man just gets up and leaves his family and doesn't care what happens to them?"

"Are you insulting me?"

"Look, this isn't about us," Amerley-mami sighed. "It's about Amerley, she needs help. She needs to be in a hospital."

"You heard Rosina, the blood is not as much as it was before.

She's getting better. In a few more weeks she'll be fine. I'm sure she just did something to provoke the boy."

"Ataa, what are you saying? What gives that boy the right to beat our daughter? What gives any man the right to beat a woman? Don't you know people go to jail for beating their spouses? And you want us to shield that spoiled boy because his parents are rich. Does Amerley need to die before you realize this is serious?"

"What do you want me to do now? I've already collected the compensation money from Mr. Iddrissu, I've used half of it for a down payment on a new outboard motor for my boat. I can't give it back."

The room went silent as the front door opened and someone walked in.

"How is she today?" I heard Mr. Iddrissu ask, and they walked into my room. I closed my eyes and pretended to sleep.

"There's less blood today. She had a little soup in the morning," Ataa said.

I opened my eyes just a little and watched them.

"She'll be fine. Don't worry," Mr. Iddrissu said, wiping his face with a handkerchief. I wondered if he'd have said the same thing if it had been Zarrah lying here instead of me.

"You know, 'boys will be boys.' If there's anything you need, don't hesitate to ask."

He slapped Ataa on the back and walked out. Ataa followed him out with an idiotic look on his face.

Amerley-mami sat on a chair by the side of my bed and began crying. The week before, she had told me what had happened. Auntie Rosina had sent for her after the assault because she couldn't be by my side 24/7 and both Priscilla and Magajia were working overtime because they had taken on my chores.

It was Amerley-mami who had taken care of me. Auntie Rosina had loaned her painkillers and sleeping pills so that for most of the first week I had been in a drug-induced haze. It was just as well because I couldn't have endured the pain otherwise. I didn't have any memories of that week.

Auntie Odarkor had moved in to stay with my sisters. Ataa had shown up unannounced one day, and she had been forced to tell him where I was and what had happened. Ataa had marched straight to the Iddrissus and insisted that I see a doctor, but it had all been a ploy. He knew that as soon as I saw a doctor, the doctor would call the police, who would then involve the Domestic Violence and Victim Support Unit, and the case would go to court. He agreed to an out-of-court settlement with the Iddrissus, which had been what he wanted all along. The Iddrissus had already paid him the compensation money he'd demanded—ten thousand cedis. Ataa thought he had gotten the better side of the deal, but I knew better. The bill for Zarrah's thirteenth birthday had come to eight thousand five hundred cedis. The money the Iddrissus had had to pay to "compensate" us had barely made a dent in their bank accounts.

I reached out and touched Amerley-mami. "It's okay," I whispered.

Amerley-mami shook her head. "No, it's not okay. You've been hurt and we're just going to pretend like nothing has happened because of money? And Rosina? She doesn't even bother coming by to see you anymore. She's making plans to move out of the country with her children, she says she can't stay with that General anymore. I wish there was someone who would fight for us. For you. I'd sell everything I have to make sure that boy is punished."

I looked at her in surprise. "Do you mean that?"

"Yes."

"You'd go against Ataa?"

"He went against us first. He left us for over a year and a half. What kind of husband or father does that to his family?"

"What about my sisters—their school and food? I'm sorry I let you down."

"Amerley, I know we're poor, but that doesn't mean we should let people treat us any way they like. And I'm the one who let you down. I'm the one who has failed you. I'm sorry. I put too much responsibility on you—the house, the girls, this job. . . . The choices *I* made have led us here today, not you. You're not to blame for anything that's happened."

I took a breath. "I know a lawyer who can help."

"But how will we pay her? Lawyers are expensive. They charge by the hour."

"Let's just talk to her. Maybe I can work for her when I get better to pay her back."

She smiled through her tears and said, "We've gone to bed on only *gari* before. We'll go to bed on only *gari* again if we have to. If I have to borrow money to get you justice, I will."

I was surprised at the words coming out of Amerley-mami's mouth, but once I was certain she was not behaving like Ataa, once I knew she really meant what she'd said about getting justice for me, I had her call Nii Okai, who carried me into the car and drove us to Auntie Fanny's house.

"**Oh my goodness!** Amerley, what happened to you?" Auntie Fanny asked as she came down the stairs. "I was in your house twice last week but Rosina wouldn't let me see you. She said you were sick. What happened?"

I was bent over. Standing up straight made my abdomen hurt more. I felt an intense burning between my legs. That was a signal I had come to know very well. It was time to pee. The pain would continue as the urine came out and would stay for a few more minutes after my bladder was empty. During those periods it was best not to even breathe.

I stood as still as a statue. I felt the warmth of the urine flow down my legs. A bloody puddle formed at my feet. I grew dizzy again and slumped against Nii Okai and Amerley-mami. Just before I blacked out, I heard Auntie Fanny shout, "Nii Okai, get her back into the car. Raul, get my purse. We're going to the hospital!"

CHAPTER 24

I sat under the cashew tree in the center of the compound house. All was quiet. The older children were in school, most of the adults were at work, and the younger kids were sprawled on a mat by my side. Fast asleep. The sun was just too hot to do anything but take a nap. I occasionally swatted away the flies that landed on their seminaked bodies. A few chickens scratched the ground, raising a cloud of dust as they foraged for food. The goats were chewing their cud under the neem tree where they were resting.

Auntie Fanny had already come to see me to prepare me for tomorrow. Tomorrow would be my first day in court. I'd have to testify against General. Once my story had appeared in the news, other girls—not just other maids who had served in the Iddrissu house but girls and women in offices and banks, schools and marketplaces, and even churches and mosques—had come out of the woodwork to accuse their rapists and abusers. They had been too scared to speak. They had been *mumus*, just like me, but in finding my voice, I'd given them a voice too.

Auntie Fanny had made me understand that what had happened had not been my fault. The fact that I had been drunk did not mean I was to blame. Rape happened when people, male or female, made a decision to hurt someone they thought they could control. She herself had been raped by someone she didn't know when she was at the university. She called me and all the other women and girls "survivors."

Rape is never ever your fault. Auntie Fanny had said it so many times that it kept playing over and over in my head. Auntie Fanny and Auntie Rosina no longer spoke to each other. Nii Okai had been fired when the Iddrissus found out he had driven me to Auntie Fanny's without permission. Priscilla quit and the agency found her a job with another family. Ataa had disappeared with all of the ten thousand cedis "compensation money."

I'd stopped peeing blood and the pain in my lower abdomen had subsided. Some days I felt fine. "Fine" in this case was not the "normal" me I had been before I moved to the Iddrissu household. That girl was gone for good; nothing would bring her back. My "fine" meant knowing that I had survived something and that I was now moving on. The days when I felt fine were few and far between.

Most days I felt like a broken egg that was still intact. Like when hens lay their eggs on the ground and the shell cracks but the pieces don't come apart, so the yolk remains intact, delicate and wobbly. I felt like if you peeled away my skin, you wouldn't find anything underneath it. Maybe you'd only find air. I felt I'd finally become invisible even to myself. The me I knew was gone. She'd disappeared. This new person who stood here pretending to be me—I had no idea who she was, but I knew I'd like her one day because she had found courage: the courage to live despite everything that had happened.

I flipped to the next page of the Bible on my lap. *Where had God been when I was being raped?* He had been right there by my side, and though I hadn't always felt him near, he had helped me survive the ordeal. I knew that the same way I knew my name was Naa Amerley Amarteifio. The same way I knew I'd get better. The same way I knew the wind existed. I had no proof. I just knew.

A taxi drove up to our door. I couldn't see who it was from where I sat. The driver sat in the car for a long time. I wondered if it was Nii Okai. Priscilla had told me he was now driving a taxi.

The driver finally got out. He walked up to our door and knocked. He tried the knob, found the door open, and stepped inside. He came out less than a minute later when he realized there was no one in there.

He put his hands on his waist and looked around. That's when he noticed me and walked over to where I sat under the cashew tree. He had kept the beard and mustache but he'd trimmed and shaped them. He was in an African print shirt and clean black corduroy pants.

"Hi," Nikoi said.

I nodded. We were both silent for a very long time. He stood there shifting his weight from one foot to the other.

Then finally he cleared his throat and said, "I heard about what happened. I'm sorry."

I nodded and looked away. The story had made headlines in news across the country. I wasn't surprised that Nikoi had heard.

"I . . . I . . . also wanted to apologize for trying to get you to change your mind even though you made it clear you didn't want to have sex until you got married. I should have respected your decision and not kept pressuring you."

I swallowed the lump that had formed in my throat, willed myself not to cry, and nodded again. I wished he would go away so I could cry and feel sorry for myself, but he still wasn't done.

"I . . . was wondering if . . . *eh* . . . if you would mind if I picked you up and drove you to court tomorrow—that's if you don't have any arrangements with anyone else. I mean even if you do have another arrangement, I'd like to drive you. It'd mean a lot to me."

Who will want her now that she's been spoiled? Nii Okai had said about the girl in the soap opera.

Inside me, I felt a tiny, tiny flutter. It was like when you light a charcoal fire and see the first tiny red glow on the smallest piece of charcoal. It would light up for just a moment and then disappear. But once you saw it, you knew that next time the glow would be larger and in no time at all you'd have a blazing fire. So you'd keep going. You'd fan that flame with all your might. You'd give it all you've got.

I looked at Nikoi. Half of my mouth lifted up in a very poor imitation of a smile. It was all I could manage for now.

"I'd like that. I'd like that very much," I said.

EPILOGUE

EIGHT YEARS LATER

I had been sitting in front of my laptop for more than an hour, staring at a document. Apart from the heading, the entire page was blank. As part of the application process for the University of Ghana School of Law, I had to upload an essay. I had begun the application process two weeks ago. I had filled in forms, uploaded copies of all my certificates, transcripts, and passport photos, and answered all the essay questions except the one I was currently staring at. I took a deep breath and began typing.

Why should you be selected for the First Degree Bachelor of Law (LLB) Program for the 2020/2021 academic year? (Max: 500 words)

Law was not even a dream I had as a child. All I wanted to be when I grew up was a seamstress with my own kiosk.

Lowly ambitions, some may say, but in a neighborhood where eight out of ten girls dropped out of school and became mothers by the age of fifteen, this was seen by almost everyone I came across as a lofty dream.

I did drop out in my first year of secondary school, not because I was pregnant but because my parents couldn't afford to pay my fees. That same year, I was sent to live with a rich aunt as a domestic worker, where I was raped by one of my mistress's sons.

In the community I grew up in, rape was always the girl's fault. Always. It was either because she had dressed too provocatively, she had gotten drunk, she was out at night when decent girls were supposed to be in their beds at home, or because she had tempted a man. Rape was the price she paid for not conforming to what society expected her to be. I believed this. For the first couple of weeks after my assault, I was too ashamed to confide in anyone. What if people thought I wasn't "good" anymore? What if by reporting the crime I had sullied my family name and ruined my sisters' future?

I was determined to keep my reputation intact, and I chose not to report the crime. One week later, that same son beat me until I became unconscious. With the help of a lawyer friend, my case was sent to court and my rapist was imprisoned.

The turning point for me, though, was when people started speaking up after my case caught the attention of the media. Girls as young as eight and women as old as sixty shared their stories. For some it was too late to get them justice, as the perpetrators had died or relocated or were untraceable. One thing we survivors all shared was the initial conviction that the assault had been our fault. That it was because of something we had done.

Today, with the help of like-minded people, I run an organization for survivors of abuse. It's hard for a victim to speak up when her abuser is the one who clothes and feeds her. At the Truth Speaks Foundation, in addition to teaching survivors vocational and entrepreneurial skills, we have on-site counselors who help them deal with their trauma and regain their sense of worth.

Like the lawyer who made sure I got the justice I deserve, I have made it my life's mission to get justice for victims of sexual and domestic abuse. I, Naa Amerley Armateifio, have decided to speak the truth, even when my voice shakes.

I read through the essay and hit the upload button to send in my application.

GLOSSARY

aba-ei   Ga for name given by porters to the Accra Metropolitan Assembly Task Force, who keep hawkers off the street. Literal meaning, "They're coming."

abom   a traditional stew made by grinding boiled *kontomire* (taro leaves), onions, and tomatoes, and adding a liberal dose of palm oil. *Koobi*, boiled eggs, and/or smoked fish are the proteins of choice. It is usually made and eaten in an *asanka* with boiled yam, plantain, cassava, or a mix of the above.

agoo/amee   local call-and-response type of greeting

akpeteshie	local gin
alasa	African cherry
apem	boiled green plantains
asanka	local name for traditional earthenware grinding bowl
banku	meal made from cooking fermented corn and cassava dough
Bo diɛŋtsɛ kwɛmɔ	Ga for "You yourself, look at what you've done"
boubou	long, loose-fitting dress
buei	expression of surprise
bɔbi tadi	dried anchovy stew
charley-wotes	flip-flops

chofi	local name for fried turkey tails
dɛɛ	local term used for emphasis
domɛdo	spiced pork that is either boiled and fried or grilled
dumsor dumsor	name given to frequent "lights-off" in Ghana
fitter	roadside mechanic
fos	used/secondhand clothing
fufu	meal made by pounding boiled plantain and cassava
galamsey	illegal gold mining
gari	roasted grated flakes of cassava
gele	elaborate Nigerian head wrap

Jeee nyɛhe sane Ga for "It's not your concern/It's none of your business"

jollof dish made from boiling rice in a meat or fish stew

juju spiritual belief system that incorporates the use of objects, such as amulets, and spells used in religious practice

kaba and slit traditional female attire consisting of a blouse, the *kaba*, and a full-length skirt, the *slit*

kanzo scorched/burnt rice

kayayo/kayayei female head porter/porters

kelewele fried spicy cubes of plantain *kenkey*

kenkey meal made from first boiling and then steaming fermented maize dough

koko	porridge made from maize flour
koobi	salted, dried tilapia fish
koose	fried bean cakes
koraa	used for emphasis
kotsa	chewing sponge used for cleaning teeth
kpakpo shitɔ	hot green pepper. Similar to Scotch bonnet pepper.
lai momo	Literally "ex-lover" in Ga, but used as a term of endearment
mami wata	mermaid
mankani cocoyam	tubers
mate	local name for a bus conductor

Me ne panin/ **Ofainɛ mi ji** **onukpa**	Twi/Ga for "I'm the older one"
mumu	local derogatory Ghanaian name for a dumb person
nketenkete	intense hunger pangs that wake one up from sleep at night
nyatse nyatse	small/young/little
Olu? Kwɛmɔ **buului anii ni ofee** **Ga**	for "Are you crazy? See the foolish thing you've done."
Osofo Maame	pastor/preacher's wife
oyibo Igbo	word used to refer to a Causasian
paa	used for emphasis

red-red   meal from boiled black-eyed beans, fried ripe plantains, and palm oil. Gets its name from the red color of the palm oil and the plantains.

saa/sɔɔ   used for emphasis

toli   a ridiculous made-up story

trotro   commercial bus

truck pusher   handcart pusher. They are usually found in markets and bus stations, where they transport various items.

tuo zaafi   meal similar to *banku* made from millet

Woaa hwɛ Twi   for "Just look"

Woasisi me   Twi for "You've cheated me"

wele   cowhide

wulomei	traditional priests
Yɛbɛwu enti yɛrenna?	Twi for "Will we refuse to sleep because of death?"
yɛyɛ	Nigerian pidgin for useless or senseless

AKPEDADA

It takes a village to birth a "book baby" and I have to say a huge thank you to the following people for helping me with the delivery: God almighty; the indefatigable Sarah Odedina and Deborah Ahenkorah of Accord Literary; the amazing team at Norton Young Readers; my brilliant editors, Jenny Jacoby and Amy Robbins; and Laylie Frazier for the gorgeous cover illustration.

Thanks to CODE's Burt Award for African Young Adult Literature for launching me on my journey.

Thanks also to my family: Mama, Dela, Eli, and OP. And to friends who have become family: Samuel Hayford, Nii Armah Tagoe, Laud Boateng, Seli Deh, Elom Yarney, Julian Sowah, Michael Avorkliyah, Ken-Edwin Aryee, Sheila Boyetey, Kwame Frimpong Boateng, and Peter Odei. Your support has been a tremendous source of encouragement.

And finally, to all my readers, akpe kakaka, which is Ewe for "Thank you so very, very much." This whole journey would be meaningless if you were not at the end of the road.

ABOUT THE AUTHOR

Ruby Yayra Goka is a dentist and a writer from Ghana. Six of her young adult books have won awards in CODE's Burt Award for African Young Adult Literature in Ghana. She lives in Accra.

ABOUT ACCORD BOOKS

Accord works with authors from across the African continent to provide support throughout the writing process and secure regional and international publishing and distribution for their works. We believe that stories are both life-affirming and life-enhancing, and want to see a world where all children are delighted and enriched by incredible stories written by African authors.